DIRE WARNING

Stanton left and Tommy got down on the floor and began petting Fred. He stopped and looked at me. "Miss Kelly, I forgot to tell you. There's something under the windshield wiper of the truck."

"Thanks for telling me." Puzzled, I left to check it out.

As I approached the vehicle, I could see a white envelope on the windshield. I pulled it out. It was soggy...probably from last night's fog. I opened it carefully so as not to rip the wet paper.

Cut out letters had been glued haphazardly. "Stop asking questions or you'll be stopped."

Simple.

To the point.

I didn't play poker, but I knew someone had just upped the ante...

T0196013

Books by Janet Finsilver

MURDER AT REDWOOD COVE

MURDER AT THE MANSION

MURDER AT THE FORTUNE TELLER'S TABLE

MURDER AT THE MUSHROOM FESTIVAL

Published by Kensington Publishing Corporation

Murder at the Mushroom Festival

Janet Finsilver

LYRICAL UNDERGROUND
Kensington Publishing Corp.
www.kensingtonbooks.com

LYRICAL UNDERGROUND BOOKS are published by

Kensington Publishing Corp.
119 West 40th Street
New York, NY 10018

All Kensington titles, imprints, and distributed lines are available at special quantity discounts for bulk purchases for sales promotion, premiums, fund-raising, educational, or institutional use.

Special book excerpts or customized printings can also be created to fit specific needs. For details, write or phone the office of the Kensington Sales Manager: Kensington Publishing Corp., 119 West 40th Street, New York, NY 10018. Attn. Sales Department. Phone: 1-800-221-2647.

Lyrical Underground and Lyrical Underground logo Reg. US Pat. & TM Off.

First Electronic Edition: April 2018
eISBN-13: 978-1-5161-0422-2
eISBN-10: 1-5161-0422-6

First Print Edition: April 2018
ISBN-13: 978-1-5161-0423-9
ISBN-10: 1-5161-0423-4

Printed in the United States of America

To my husband, E. J., who has always been beside me during this writing journey.

Acknowledgments

My husband, E. J., continues to help me on my writing path. He's my expert when it comes to anything about vehicles. My great writing group made up of Colleen Casey, Staci McLaughlin, Ann Parker, Carole Price, and Penny Warner gave me wonderful feedback, and we had a lot of fun along the way. I really appreciated the comments I received from my beta readers, Cyndie Bell and Linda Uhrenholt. Their input was very helpful. Mario Abreu, staff naturalist at the Mendocino Coast Botanical Gardens, taught me an enormous amount about mushrooms. A warm thank you goes out to my agent, Dawn Dowdle, and my editor, John Scognamiglio, for what they do on my behalf. Thank you all!

Chapter 1

Mushrooms of all shapes, sizes, and colors covered the top of the large table in the work area of Redwood Cove Bed-and-Breakfast. Each had been centered on a white piece of paper. Some looked like a person's sweet, peaceful dream of fluffy white clouds. Others were from someone's ghoulish nightmare. I reached toward a fascinating orange one with white dots.

"Stop!" the short, blond woman next to me shouted.

I quickly pulled my hand back.

The woman put her camera on the table. "I'm sorry to startle you. That one, as are some of the others, is poisonous, and you can absorb the toxins through your skin. Contrary to popular belief, you don't risk dying unless you ingest them, but you might have a nasty allergic reaction."

"You don't have to apologize for keeping me from getting sick," I told the photographer, Elise Jenkins.

She laughed. "Thanks for letting me do my mushroom class at your inn."

"I'm looking forward to learning about them as well as finding out more about the Mushroom Festival. As the new manager here, the more I know, the more I can inform my guests."

"It's a lot of fun. I've been going to the festival's events for years. Among other things, there are demonstrations, special menus at many of the restaurants, and a contest. I grew up here and the start of mushroom season is something I look forward to every year, along with many of the other locals."

"You said some of these are poisonous. I've heard eating wild mushrooms can be dangerous."

"It can be. You really need to know what you're doing and not take any chances if you're not sure. People still die, even though they know they need to be careful. There's a saying that goes, 'There are old mushroom hunters and bold mushroom hunters but rarely someone who is both.'"

Elise put on rubber gloves, began picking up certain mushrooms and double-bagging them in plastic bags. She placed them in an ice chest. "I'll take these home with me. I'll leave the others here to show at the lunch later. Those on that side of the table are safe to touch." She pointed to the left.

I picked up one that looked like a dozen miniature fans glued together in an overlapping pattern to form a mushroom tower. The fungus felt soft and rubbery.

"That's called the hen of the woods," Elise said.

I turned the tan cluster in a number of different directions, but couldn't see any resemblance to the chickens on my parents' ranch.

Elise put the chest in a corner and then pulled name cards out of her briefcase. She began placing them on a long, narrow display table next to the wall.

"I'm going to put the mushrooms over here and keep the display up for the identification portion of the class. We'll be needing the table for eating and food preparation."

I put the hen down above her name tag.

The sound of a car in the driveway drew my attention out the window of the inn's back door. A four-door sedan rolled to a stop. A silver-haired, nattily dressed gentleman in a tweed jacket and cap emerged from a classic gold Mercedes. Herbert Winthrop, better known as the Professor from his days at UC Berkeley, had arrived.

A white Prius and a green pickup with a camper shell drove in behind him and parked. The drivers of the other vehicles emerged, both wearing long-sleeved shirts, blue jeans, and hiking boots. One wore a bright red cap with a matching scarf around his neck. The Professor had informed the Silver Sentinels, a crime-solving group of senior citizens of which he was a member and I had honorary status, that his younger brother and one of his friends was coming to the Mushroom Festival and attending the class at the inn.

They walked up the back steps and knocked on the door.

"Hi," I greeted them as I opened it for them.

A breath of salty ocean air followed them in.

The Professor took off his cap and nodded at me. "Good to see you, my dear." He turned to the two who had followed him in. "I'd like to introduce you to my brother, Timothy." He pointed to a slim man with a strong family resemblance who had the Professor's same sparkling blue eyes.

Timothy extended his hand. "I've heard a lot about you. It's great to finally meet you."

"Same here," I said, and we did the customary handshake.

His hand was soft, but his grip was firm.

Indicating the rotund man next to Timothy, the Professor said, "And this is his friend, Clarence Norton."

He stepped forward. "Hi!" His neat mustache had the whisper of a curl at the ends and his full head of gray hair was brushed back.

I received a vigorous handshake.

"I'm so excited to be here! This class sounds like it'll be great." A laugh punctuated the sentence.

"Timothy and Clarence, this is Kelly Jackson, manager of Redwood Cove Bed-and-Breakfast," the Professor said.

"It's nice to meet you both. Welcome to the inn and please come in." I closed the door and joined them. "This is our multipurpose room. It contains a work space on the left, a kitchen on the right, and a living area at the far end." The spacious room was the hub of our activities and always had a welcoming feel about it.

Elise moved the last mushroom from the table.

"This is your instructor, Elise Jenkins." I nodded in her direction and introduced them.

"Hi, everyone," she said. "I look forward to working with you. I'm about ready to prepare lunch, so we'll talk more later."

The men said hi, and Clarence and Timothy told her how much they were looking forward to the class.

"Professor, I know you're not taking the class," Elise said, "but you're welcome to join us for lunch. I have plenty of food."

"I'd love to, Ms. Jenkins. That's a kind offer."

"Please, call me Elise."

"So I shall," he replied.

I led them to the living area where there was a couch and chairs. "Please, have a seat. Would anyone like some coffee or tea?"

"I'd like some coffee," Clarence said.

Timothy and the Professor responded in the negative.

"Would you like cream and sugar?" I asked Clarence.

"Yes, my sweet tooth just won't leave me alone," he chuckled.

I went to the kitchen and prepared Clarence's coffee, handed it to him, and sat down with the three men.

"We're really looking forward to the event," said Timothy. "We've spent two years learning about mushrooms."

I settled back into my chair. "That's a long time. What made you decide to do that?"

Clarence shifted his position, but it was almost more of a bounce up and down. "We compete every two years in an area we choose. We work to learn as much as we can and see who can be the best."

Timothy picked up the conversation. "We chose mushrooms this time. I knew about the festival and the contest, and it sounded like fun."

Clarence pulled his red wool scarf off and pointed to his matching cap. "Last time our area of expertise was knitting."

"Knitting?" I asked.

Timothy laughed. "Yes. The knitting club in Berkeley where I live didn't bat an eye."

Clarence grinned. "On the other hand, quite a few eyebrows shot up when I walked into a meeting of the Minnesota Knitters Guild. Once I explained, they were really good sports about it. I didn't realize I had ten thumbs."

"Who won?" I asked.

"Two ladies from each group judged our creations. We shipped them back and forth. They declared it a tie."

"Why knitting?"

They both shrugged.

"We did it on a whim." Clarence chuckled. "We were looking through a class catalogue to get ideas. We saw a knitting class and decided that would be new and different."

Elise leaned over the counter that divided the kitchen and work area. "Gentlemen, you're welcome to look at the mushrooms on the table. They're all labeled."

While the three men went to check them out, I joined Elise in the kitchen, where she was beginning to prepare the welcome lunch. "Is there anything I can do to help?"

Savory smells had begun to fill the air.

"If you'd set the table, that would be wonderful. I'm not familiar with where the dishes and silverware are kept."

"Sure." I pulled out plates from the cupboard.

I knew from the paperwork I'd seen there were eight participants, six staying at the inn. Elise had asked me to join the class whenever possible, and I was attending today's session. I added three plates for Elise, myself, and the Professor.

Elise opened a black nylon case on the counter. It contained a variety of knives.

I took the plates to the table. "Whatever you're making smells divine."

"Mushroom quiche to help get us into the swing of things. The class is about identifying and finding mushrooms as well as cooking them. This is a recipe I created using a lot of local wild herbs. I prepared the quiches at home and only need to heat them." She selected one of the knives and put it on a cutting board. "Kelly, thank you again for hosting my class here at your inn. I lost my job as a chef, and it's a challenge to make ends meet."

"I'm sorry to hear that. I'm glad I can be of help."

Elise pulled a huge salad bowl of greens from the refrigerator as well as bags of produce. "My mother's in an assisted care home. My son, Joey, helps as much as he can with the bills. He's a woodworker with limited resources. Joey teaches part-time at a craft school and builds redwood tables he sells in a local art gallery."

I added silverware to the table settings.

"I've been working odd jobs here and there. I hope to get something soon." She began chopping a yellow bell pepper. "Roger Simmons, the sponsor of the mushroom contest, bought the restaurant I worked at. The property is adjacent to his estate. The owners hadn't planned on selling for a couple more years, but he just kept offering them more money. They eventually sold."

"Is it still a restaurant?" I asked.

"No. He just wanted the property. There's a spectacular ocean view. He gutted the building, put in an art studio for his work, and built an addition of a small warehouse. Roger works with wood and that takes a lot of equipment."

I was learning about another aspect of Redwood Cove. I'd seen some of the redwood items for sale but didn't know much about the process for creating them.

"He was very generous to all the employees. We had a lot of notice, and he gave us severance pay that was more than any of us expected. The owners are now very well set for their retirement. I'm unemployed right now, but I don't feel any ill will toward him." She tossed the pepper into the salad bowl.

I finished setting the table. "Mr. Simmons called and said he wanted to meet me. He's coming over in a little bit."

Elise wiped her hands on a dish towel. "He visits as many of the mushroom activities as he can."

She pulled appetizers from the refrigerator and uncovered them. I arranged them on the counter. The men joined us.

"Help yourself," she said as she placed them on the table. "The others should be arriving soon."

I picked up one of the stuffed mushrooms and bit into it. The filling melted in my mouth with a tangy cheese flavor and the taste of dill. I detected a hint of garlic and other spices I couldn't identify.

Clarence picked up an appetizer and beamed at Elise. "I can't wait to get into the woods and start the hunt."

"Me, too," Timothy said. "It's so gorgeous here. The combination of the redwood forests and the Pacific Ocean makes for stunning views. We have fun events planned as well as being in a breathtaking area."

Elise frowned. "The woods are indeed beautiful, but they can also be dangerous, a place of mystery and darkness." She put another plate of appetizers out. "People have been known to get killed in these woods."

Chapter 2

The excitement in their faces slipped away and fear entered.

Clarence stepped toward Elise. "Killed? Why?"

"A number of reasons. There are people living deep in the woods who don't want to be found. They have their secrets to protect. Illegal drug activity is another. A keep-out sign means exactly that. And, of course, the mountain lions."

"Mountain lions?" Timothy's voice had taken on a high-pitched note.

Elise put pitchers of tea on the granite kitchen divider. "For the most part they stay away from people. But there have been some incidents. Especially if a lion's been injured or has cubs."

She left the kitchen and went to a pile of papers on the side table, where the mushrooms were, and returned with some stapled sheets. Elise handed one to Clarence and the other to Timothy.

"Here are maps of hunting locations. If you follow my directions and use the maps, you'll be fine and have a lot of fun. I didn't mean to scare you, but I did want to stress it's important to be careful. I can tell you're really excited, and I heard you mention a competition. I didn't want you to get carried away in the heat of the contest."

The Professor looked over Timothy's shoulder at the papers he held. "Who knew hunting fungi could be life threatening? My new piece of knowledge for the day."

A car drove by the side window of the work area. I didn't know much about types of vehicles, but I knew my animals and recognized another type of big cat in the hood ornament—a leaping jaguar. The black car parked, and a man with dark brown hair parted on the side got out. He headed along the walk toward the front of the inn.

I walked down the hallway to greet him, the sounds of my steps muffled by an oriental runner.

I opened the door before he had time to knock. "Welcome. I'm Kelly Jackson."

"Roger Simmons," he responded. "Pleased to meet you."

The sweet scent of the profusion of red, yellow, and blue flowers covering the vines climbing the porch railing drifted in.

"The mushroom class is being held in our multipurpose room in the back. Come this way."

Roger wore a light tan sports coat and neatly creased navy slacks. A silk scarf tucked in his breast pocket had a pattern with colors perfectly matching his attire. He was tall and substantial in size.

We joined the others and everyone exchanged names except for Elise, who gave the newcomer a wave.

Roger looked at me. "Thank you for participating in the Mushroom Festival. The more activities we can offer, the better for attracting people."

"I've been reading about it in the newspaper," I said. "There certainly is a variety of events to choose from."

Roger nodded. "You're right. People really get into it. It goes for two weeks. The chefs outdo themselves coming up with new recipes for breakfast, lunch, and dinner."

Elise chimed in. "Including dessert."

"Dessert? Mushroom dessert?" I laughed. "I don't know if I'm ready for that."

Elise smiled. "I wouldn't decide too fast. Wait until you try the candy cap mushroom ice cream."

"There's more," Roger said. "Locals lead hikes to find and identify mushrooms. A stable arranged a special horseback ride and a company called Paddler's Paradise has organized a canoe trip. You can walk, ride, or paddle to find fungi."

Elise pointed to the table with the mushrooms. "There are lists and flyers for the activities if you want to look at them over there." The Professor, Timothy, and Clarence went over to investigate and began picking up various papers.

"Any luck finding a job, Elise?" Roger asked.

Her back stiffened slightly. "Not yet. But something will come along."

"I'll let you know if I hear of anything," Roger said.

"Thanks." She sighed and returned to putting beverages on the counter. "Would you like to join us for lunch?"

"Thanks for the offer, but I'll have to pass. I have another appointment."

"Okay. I know this is a busy time for you," Elise replied.

He turned to me. "I understand you're new to the area. I'd love to have you come and see my art studio. I open it once a month to the public, and your guests might like to know about it. I'll give you a private tour."

"I'd like that. Elise said you create pieces using redwood. I know the trees are an important part of this area, and I'd like to learn more about what people do with them."

He pulled out his wallet, extracted a card, and handed it to me. "Excellent. I'll show you my woodworking equipment and walk you through the process. It's not a side of the craft I have many opportunities to talk about with people."

I examined the card—smooth black cardstock with his name and phone number in elegant, silver lettering. "I'll be in touch."

"I look forward to hearing from you," Roger said.

A battered yellow pickup truck drove by and parked.

"Oh, it's Peter Smith," Elise said. "I forgot to tell you about him, Kelly. I invited him to join us for lunch. He's won the contest for the last five years, and I think he can add some interesting information."

Elise had seen where the plates and utensils were kept and set another place at the table. A couple of class members wandered in and she went to greet them.

I opened the back door and called out, "Mr. Smith," as the man with sparse sandy hair locked his pickup. "This is where the class is meeting."

He trotted up the back stairs. Peter was a little shorter than me, which made him about five foot four. He wore blue jeans almost faded to white and a red-and-white-checked flannel shirt. His scruffy sneakers appeared to have been on more than one muddy walk. Light gray eyes showed behind the light brown translucent frames of his glasses.

"I'm Kelly Jackson, manager here. Elise told me your name when she saw you drive by."

"Nice to meet you." He gave me a thin-lipped smile.

Clarence came hustling by. "I'm going to get our notepads and the books we bought for the class. Would you like to meet Max?" he asked me.

I was momentarily startled. Had someone been sitting outside in the car this whole time?

Clarence saw my look. "Maximilian, Max for short, is my mushroom-hunting dog."

"Sure. I wouldn't want to miss a chance to make a new canine friend."

Peter inched a bit in our direction, a slight frown on his face.

I followed Clarence down the steps, Roger and Peter behind us. Roger took out his car keys as Clarence opened the back of his camper shell. A quivering bundle of silky soft, golden curls greeted me as I reached in to pet him. Dark brown eyes peered at me through tendrils of hair. He had a medium-sized body and long legs.

"When I got Max from a rescue group, they guessed he was a mix of golden retriever, lab, and maybe water dog because of the curly hair. All good sniffers, making him a good candidate for finding fungi."

Max had a big grin and an even bigger tail wag going on. His thick tail whacked the side of the vehicle, creating a fast-paced drum beat.

"He's really good at finding mushrooms, though I think Portia is a little better." Clarence scratched behind the dog's ears. "Unfortunately, I couldn't find a place that would let me bring a dog as well as a potbellied pig."

Roger had joined in petting the dog. "I've heard of mushroom-hunting pigs."

"They're used a lot in Europe and can smell truffles as far down as three feet. There's documentation of their use that goes back centuries. However, dogs are preferred overall. Mushroom hunters like to keep their areas secret, and that's a lot harder with a grunting pig. It's also a challenge to haul a four-hundred-pound animal around unless you have a truck…and not all mushroom hunters drive pickups."

Roger rubbed Max's ears. The dog gave a low groan and leaned into Roger's sports coat. He didn't seem to mind.

"Always wanted to have a little farm and a variety of animals," Clarence said. "When I moved to Oregon a little over a year ago, I found the perfect place. Since Timothy and I had our competition going, I thought I'd start with a dog and a pig and train them to find fungi."

Peter had been creeping closer and closer. Now he stood next to Clarence, a scowl on his face.

He glanced at Max. "Nice looking dog, but you can't use it in the contest."

Clarence's chin jutted forward the slightest bit. "Yes, I can."

Peter's hands balled into fists. "No, you can't."

His voice had gone up several decibels. Peter's complexion had reddened and his nostrils flared. He thrust his face closer to Clarence's.

Clarence's chin was out as far as it would go. "Yes, I can. I checked the rules and there's nothing in them about not using an animal."

Peter responded by mimicking Clarence's posture. "No, you can't."

We had dueling chins. If they'd been pistols, I would've expected them to walk ten paces away from each other, turn, and shoot.

The mushroom-hunting lark had flown in an unexpected direction. I never thought I'd hear about people being killed in the woods or see someone about to fly into a rage. What next?

Chapter 3

Roger stepped up next to the two men. "Gentlemen, we have a Mushroom Festival committee. They'll decide about using the dog."

"But it starts tomorrow," Peter sputtered.

"Not a problem. They're meeting with me this afternoon to go over the final details. Peter, I have your contact information. Mr. Norton, what's the best way for me to reach you?"

Clarence pulled out a card and handed it to Roger. "This has my cell phone number on it. I understand there are areas where they don't get reception here. If you have trouble getting ahold of me, I'm staying at the Blue Heron Inn. You can leave a message for me there. And, of course, I'm here for lunch as well as cooking later this afternoon."

Roger carefully placed the card in his wallet. "I'm familiar with that inn. I'll let you know what the decision is."

Peter wasn't going to let it go. "But…but…but he can't."

Roger looked at him and inclined his head toward his car. "Walk with me."

I went over to give the dog a last pet.

Roger's voice drifted back to me. "Peter, that temper of yours could get you in serious trouble again. Someone might figure they've had enough of it, and there'll be an unhappy outcome."

Clarence came over, scratched Max behind the ears, and closed the back of the camper shell. "I certainly didn't expect that."

"Some people don't deal with surprises well, especially when there's a contest involved," I said.

We walked up the steps of the back porch. As I entered the work area, I wondered what kind of trouble Peter had been in.

I went to check phone messages and saw Elise point Clarence to one of the three empty chairs. The rest of the class participants had arrived and were chatting with each other.

When I finished, I joined the group and Elise directed me to a seat beside a man I hadn't met. He was talking to Clarence, who was sitting on his other side. I seated myself next to the newcomer. The uniform color of his black hair made me suspect he dyed it. A worn leather notebook rested next to his right hand. I could see part of a name embossed on its spine, but not all the letters were discernable.

He turned to me. "Hello, I'm Ned Blaine."

His dark eyes were magnified behind thick black-rimmed glasses. His pencil-thin black mustache mirrored the shape of the top of his eyeglass frames.

"Kelly Jackson. I'm the manager here."

"Nice to meet you. I asked Elise to seat me next to you if possible. I'm a reporter for the *Redwood Cove Messenger* and wanted to ask you some questions. I know you're new to the area and you've made some changes here. I'd like to schedule an appointment to hear about them and learn more about you."

"Great. When we're done here, I'll get out my calendar."

Peter entered and took the remaining seat. His face had returned to the pale color I'd seen when he arrived. He scowled in our direction. I figured it was for Clarence, though his gaze seemed to be on Ned.

Elise stood. "Thank you, everyone, for joining the class and signing up for the mushroom contest. We'll be doing some fungi hunting this afternoon. The main prize this year is for the largest variety of mushrooms found. In addition, there will be a prize for the most artistic collecting basket and a new one called Judge's Choice."

Ned took notes as Elise talked.

"We have a full afternoon ahead of us," Elise said, "starting with lunch…a mushroom-themed one, of course."

She went on to talk about what was in the quiches and the appetizers. Two large bowls of salad had been placed on either end of the table. As people helped themselves, Elise delivered plates with two types of quiches, bright yellow and red cherry tomatoes, and a number of colorful flowers. Bright red blossoms intermingled with orange ones, and thin curling green strips of vegetation circled the edge of the plates. Squash blossoms, purple lilacs, and dark blue pansies rested next to the main course.

Elise held up a paper. "Everything on your plate is edible. You'll find next to your plate a photo and description of each item as well as recipes for the quiches."

"This looks gorgeous, Elise," I said.

"Thanks, Kelly." Pink colored her cheeks. "Everyone, there's more quiche. I'll leave it on the counter, and you can help yourself if you want more."

Appreciative murmurs filled the room as people began to eat. I took a bite of each quiche and was surprised at the distinct difference in taste. They looked very similar. One had an earthy taste and large slices of mushrooms rested in the creamy custard mixture. The other one had notably more herbs and small chunks of fungi. There were other flavors I couldn't identify.

I'd never eaten flowers before, but I was always game to try something new. As I tried an orange one, I scanned the handout. I discovered it was a nasturtium. Its flavor was sweet and peppery. I recognized the lilac and nibbled on it while enjoying its fragrant scent and lemony taste. Sweet pea tendrils created attractive slender green curlicues. I grazed my way through lunch.

I sat back and Ned caught my eye. "Would it be possible for you to tell me now a little about the changes you've made?"

"Sure," I replied.

Ned opened his notebook and pulled a pen from a holder inside.

"There's only one overall change I've made. I created a theme for each room."

"Can you give me an example?"

"One is called the puzzle and game room. There's a large jigsaw puzzle guests can work on, set up on a table. There are smaller ones a person could finish during a weekend stay. I have antique puzzle boxes that are decorative and can be a challenge to figure out. There is also a variety of well-known board games as well as some unusual ones from the Victorian era."

Ned was taking notes in small, precise, cursive handwriting. No time or energy lost with large loops. "Interesting. Do you find people ask for particular rooms?"

"Absolutely. We have a lot of pictures and descriptions online. It's rare that a person hasn't made a choice before calling."

"Where did you find the furnishings?"

"Antique stores, garage sales, arts and crafts stores. I started looking as soon as my boss, Michael Corrigan, the owner of Resorts International, the company that owns this inn, approved the idea. There was a renovation planned before I started as manager, so the timing was good to make changes. When I was hired, I went back home to get my things. I found a number of items in Jackson, Wyoming, near where I lived on my parents' cattle and guest ranch. I shopped my way across the states as I drove here. It'll be a fun work in progress for a while to come."

Ned nodded and closed his notebook. "It sounds like an innovative idea. I'd like to do a couple of articles. One specifically about the inn and the rooms and one about you being new to Redwood Cove and how you feel about it."

"Wonderful!"

It would be a great opportunity for advertising the bed-and-breakfast as well as an opportunity for people to learn about the changes.

Ned turned to Clarence and they engaged in conversation as I finished my lunch. Every so often Peter cast a frown in our direction. People settled back in their chairs with contented sighs and empty plates. Elise and I cleared the dishes as people conversed.

"Class," Elise said when we were finished, "I'd like to introduce you to Peter Smith. He's won the contest the last five years, is very knowledgeable about all things mushroom, and has agreed to help answer questions you might have."

Peter stood. "Thanks, Elise. The lunch was outstanding. Your culinary talents continue to delight and amaze those fortunate enough to taste your creations."

Once again a rosy glow graced her cheeks. It was nice to see Peter had a pleasant side.

"The contest is a lot of fun." He raised his eyebrows and cocked his head at the group. "I'm happy to assist Elise. However, I'm out for win number six Saturday. I'll be at the starting line waiting for the sound of the shot with all of you. The race will be on when the pistol fires."

For the next hour, Elise instructed the class in the art of mushroom hunting. We learned about different types of fungi with names like milk cap, pig's ear, lobster, and cauliflower. The latter indeed looked like a big, brown head of the vegetable. Peter chimed in on occasion.

Elise held up a stack of papers. "Here are the directions for where we're going to take a mushroom walk. I'd like to meet there in half an hour. We'll work as a group for an hour and then you'll be on your own." She passed out the information. "Remember to dress warmly. Redwood Cove can get quite chilly, especially if the fog comes in. Also, the woods can be very damp and muddy, so wear appropriate shoes."

The inn's guests departed for their rooms. The Professor, Timothy, and Clarence went out to take Max for a walk. I made an appointment with Ned then helped Elise clean up. Ned sat down at the counter that separated the kitchen from the work area. He opened his notebook and took out a pen.

Peter came over and planted himself next to Ned, arms crossed, feet apart. "There's talk all over town about what you've been up to. People don't like it."

Ned looked up at him in an unhurried way. "And just what is it you're talking about?"

The red returned to Peter's face. "Don't give me that. You know darn well what I'm talking about. The book you're putting together on where to find mushrooms. The articles you're selling on the Internet giving away the location of people's hunting areas."

"Everything I've written about is on *public* land." Ned raised his pen and brought it down in a decisive movement, like a band conductor emphasizing a certain note with a baton, when he used the word *public*. It stopped a couple of inches from Peter's chest like a jabbing finger. "The *public* has a right to know what's out there."

"If you weren't spying on people, following them, you wouldn't know about those places. The whereabouts of some of those patches have been passed down through generations. A number of families rely on those mushrooms as part of their income. You know as well as I do how difficult it can be for some people to make a living up here."

"As I said, it's *public* land." Up went his arm and down again. Another explosive note. "The *public* has a right to know. It's the *public's* land."

Peter put his face close to Ned's, almost nose to nose. "I'd sure better not find anything about my places on your website, or else."

Ned held his ground. "Or else what?"

"You'd better hope you never find out." Peter barged past Ned. Windows rattled as the door slammed.

Chapter 4

Anger management issues for sure. Ned seemed unperturbed. I looked at the caramel-colored, tooled leather cover of his notebook. It reminded me of my saddle in the storage shed. Suddenly I yearned to get some riding in at the local stable. I had yet to ride on the beach. I shook my head and brought myself back to the present.

"That's nice workmanship." I pointed to the cover.

Ned reached out and ran his finger over the worn leather. "Thanks. My older brother made it for me. He was a captain in the army and was killed in battle. It keeps him close to me."

I thought of my own family and how difficult it would be if I lost one of my brothers. "I'm sorry to hear about your loss. I know about items that keep family with us. Mine put together a special cowboy hat for me when I began working here. Everyone contributed something to its creation."

Ned nodded. "Nice."

Elise had put the leftovers in the refrigerator and was almost finished cleaning the dishes.

I walked over to her. "I'm going to get my jacket and change my shoes for the mushroom hunt. It seemed like everyone loved your food and enjoyed the talk."

"I think so, too. I saw a lot of smiles throughout the afternoon."

I walked down the hallway to my rooms. When I opened the door, I felt like I was stepping outside. The huge glass windows directly in front of me framed the dazzling blue Pacific Ocean in the distance. Waves broke and scattered spray over the outcroppings of rock. Garden flowers filled the equally large window on my right and gave me ongoing opportunities for bird watching. The window seat was my favorite place to sit. The person who built this room had given its occupants a phenomenal gift.

I went into the bedroom, changed clothes, and pulled my red hair back into a ponytail. Retrieving a bottle of Pellegrino from the galley-sized kitchen, I paused a moment and thought about making an espresso from the commercial-size coffeemaker. My boss loved a good cup of coffee and made sure all the staff had opportunities to enjoy it as well. Glancing at the clock, I decided I didn't have enough time.

When I entered the multipurpose room, I saw Daniel Stevens, manager of a sister property, chatting with Elise. Redwood Cove was a small town and pretty much anyone who had lived there for a long time knew each other. Daniel had his hand on a box on the counter. We shared duties, such as ordering produce and arranging for deliveries.

I joined them and nodded at the box. "Hi, Daniel. What's up?"

"I brought over your portion of the fruit that came in. Dry goods are being delivered early tomorrow morning, and I'll bring them over then."

His high cheekbones, straight ebony hair tied in a ponytail, and light brown skin left no doubt as to his Native American heritage.

"There's no rush. It can wait until after breakfast is taken care of."

"Allie has been taking my place for breakfast delivery on the weekends. She earns a little extra money, and I think she likes being involved. It's a three-day weekend, so she is home tomorrow. There's no problem with me leaving Ridley House."

Allie, his eighth-grade daughter, had the same lustrous black hair and tan complexion.

The Professor, his brother, and his friend came in.

I waved them over to join us. "Timothy and Clarence, I'd like you to meet Daniel Stevens. He manages Ridley House."

They exchanged handshakes and greetings.

Daniel handed me a list of what was in the box. "Kelly, I'm going to a special place I know to pick chanterelles this afternoon. It's on sacred Native American land and has beautiful views. Would you like to come with me?"

"I'd love to. I'm only staying for the first hour of Elise's class when she's going to walk with us. After that people will be on their own."

"Okay. I'll come by to pick you up. What time?"

"Elise, what time do you think I could be back here?"

"About two forty-five."

"That works for me," Daniel said.

"Great! I'll see you then."

Elise picked up her purse. "Time to go."

The Professor addressed his guests. "I'll meet you back here. The Silver Sentinels have a meeting in the inn's conference room this afternoon."

Timothy said, "Okay," and he and Clarence headed out.

I retrieved the keys to the red Toyota pickup with Redwood Cove Bed-and-Breakfast painted on the side. I had decided to use it when I felt there was an opportunity to advertise, and the festival certainly qualified. Putting the map on the seat, I decided it would be easier to follow Elise, who pulled out ahead of me in a brown Chevrolet sedan.

It took a little over ten minutes to arrive at the California national park area indicated in the directions. The rest of the group had assembled in the parking lot. Elise and I joined them.

Elise held up pictures of the mushrooms we might find. She explained that particular trees attracted certain fungi. The mushrooms were actually the fruit of a large underground organism. When hunters found a certain fungi area, they would return to it because more would be produced.

We began walking on dirt paths in a redwood forest of soaring trees reaching for the sky. After only a couple of feet, Elise stopped. Pointing to several mushrooms, she identified them as black trumpets. A few more steps and I found myself looking at a white growth that turned out to be matsutakes. Now that my attention was on mushrooms, I was astounded by how many I saw. Who knew the world was populated by so many different varieties? When you began to focus on something, it was amazing what you saw.

Within fifteen minutes, the group had found six different types. One woman was the proud "owner" of a very large King Bolete, otherwise known as a porcini. Elise recognized it because of its very distinctive shape and told her it was safe to eat.

At a huge tree stump about ten feet in diameter, Elise stopped. "Almost all of the original growth trees were logged years ago. What you see are second- and third-generation trees."

The rest of the hour passed quickly.

"That's it for our group foraging. We'll meet back at the inn at four thirty. We're making candy cap ice cream and cupcakes for tomorrow's dessert."

I wasn't convinced that the words *mushrooms* and *dessert* should be combined, but I'd give it a try. I drove back to the bed-and-breakfast to meet Daniel.

His faded Volkswagen bus was parked in the lot. The engine knocked a bit, but it kept on going. Daniel was proud of its all-original status and kept it immaculate.

He was at the counter with Helen Rogers, the inn's baker and assistant, sipping a cup of coffee. Helen and her young son lived on site in a small cottage.

"How did the mushroom hunting go?" Daniel asked.

"I was amazed at how many I saw when they were the focus of my attention. It makes me wonder what I miss as I walk through life."

"I know what you mean," he said. "Are you ready to go?"

"Yes, I'm looking forward to seeing more of the area."

Helen stood and put her cup down. She pushed back her gray-streaked hair, twisted it into a bun, and clasped it with a clip she pulled from her pocket. "I'm getting an early start on tonight's appetizers, so I'll be pretty much out of the way when the class returns."

"Good thinking. Elise really appreciates our hosting her class. She's had some tough times lately with losing her job."

"She seems like a nice lady. I hope things change for her soon." Helen opened the refrigerator and took out a brick of cheese.

Daniel and I went out the back and walked to his bus. He opened the passenger door for me, and I settled in on the worn but clean vinyl seat. He started it, and we rattled our way down the driveway.

"As I said earlier, the place I'm taking you to is sacred to my tribe. It has spiritual meaning to us."

"Thank you for sharing it with me. You said you were going for chanterelles. Are you into mushroom hunting?"

He shook his head. "No, I don't know enough and don't really have a strong interest in it. Some of the poisonous ones and the safe ones can look very similar. Chanterelles are easy to recognize. This area produces a lot of them."

We passed a sign for Mallory National Park, then Daniel pulled off the highway onto what was almost a dirt track, not a road. We bumped along the twisting path for about five minutes. He parked, and we got out in what I felt was an enchanted forest. I breathed in the life of the woodland around me. Musty, sweet, earthy, topped off with a sprinkling of salt from the nearby ocean. Spears of sunlight cut through the towering redwoods like beacons to highlight certain areas. A raven cawed, loud and raucous, as we walked through a sunlit glen. A hawk drifted overhead, soaring on the wind currents.

Now that my consciousness was on Mother Earth, I not only saw a multitude of mushrooms but a vast variety of flowers. I thanked nature for such a wondrous place and reveled in my enhanced awareness.

Daniel led me to an area that looked down on a river with translucent water. I saw the backs of the birds flying below us.

He had brought a basket, and he led me around, showing me where the mushrooms we sought were popping up. It didn't take us long to fill the container with spongy fungi. We went back to the overlook.

"That's the Carson River. If you look carefully into it, you'll see a gigantic, submerged old-growth redwood log."

I made out the faint line of the log under the rippling water.

He handed me the binoculars he'd been carrying around his neck. "I brought these because I thought you might enjoy getting a closer look."

I held them up and looked at the huge section of tree trunk. It leapt to life through the lenses.

"The log is immense. How big do you think it is?"

"It's probably about twenty feet in diameter and over fifty feet in length. The loggers had to cut the big ones in pieces to take them out. It's called a sinker log, and it's from the logging operations of the mid–eighteen hundreds. That log is worth a lot of money."

"Why?"

"The old-growth redwoods are very dense and tight grained. In addition, the sinker logs have unusual colors like blond and burgundy, resulting from having been in the mineral-rich water of the river. It's jackpot time for fine woodworkers if they can locate some. They're illegal to harvest now without a permit. Everybody I know who has requested one has been turned down, so it's rare when any comes on the market."

"How does any of it become available then, if it's against the law to retrieve them?"

"There are some stashes from when it was legal to take them. And… people continue to harvest them. There's black market redwood. The loggers come in at night with heavy equipment. There have been some accidents from chains snapping and cranes overturning." He shook his head. "The need or greed for money. People have been killed pulling up this timber."

Chapter 5

Daniel unlocked the bus and put the basket of mushrooms behind the driver's seat. "After I drop you off, I'm going to pick up Allie and Tommy and take them to my place. They want to work on their homework together."

"It's so great they've teamed up."

Tommy, Helen's ten-year-old son, had Asperger's, and he'd had a hard time fitting in when he and his mom moved to Redwood Cove.

"He's a whiz at math and science," Daniel said. "He's done wonders for Allie's new success in those subjects at school. She's reading more for fun as well. Helen and I are taking them to the school's book fair tomorrow night."

Daniel pulled out onto the highway and drove under a canopy of soaring redwoods. Fingers of golden light reached through the trees and pointed to a lush green fern here and a brilliant cluster of red flowers there, as if not wanting us to miss nature's treats.

I pulled my gaze away from the entrancing scenery and looked at Daniel. "It's sweet how protective she is of him."

"Oh, yeah. She's a no-nonsense kid. The bullies at school know to stay away from him now."

The tall thirteen-year-old was a force to be reckoned with.

Daniel took the turn off for the inn, drove into the parking lot, and stopped next to the inn's truck.

"That was fun," I said as I got out. "Thanks for showing me the area and teaching me about sinker logs."

"You bet. Happy to do it. I'll be back in a bit with the kids."

"Okay."

Helen was in the kitchen area covering trays of cheese with plastic wrap. Elise stood at the worktable putting out brushes.

I went over and picked one up. It was about six inches long with stiff bristles.

"Hi, Kelly." Elise pulled another brush from a pouch she had on a chair. "Those are what you use to clean mushrooms. You don't want to run them under water because they absorb too much liquid."

"My mom taught me that years ago. I used to help her in the kitchen." I put the brush down. "I'm going to go check on a meeting and then I'll come back and help you set up."

"Thanks for the offer. There's not much to do. The class will be cleaning and preparing the mushrooms."

As I walked down the hallway, I heard voices from the conference room. I turned and went to see what was happening. I paused at the entrance and read the name over the door—THE SILVER SENTINELS' ROOM. The word *silver* was for their shared hair color and *sentinels* for the watch they kept over their community. I entered and saw the namesakes of the room busy sorting piles of photographs.

"Hi, everyone," I said.

Gertrude Plumber, "Gertie" for short, sat on the far side of the table facing the entrance. She looked up from the neat piles arranged in front of her. "Hello, Kelly."

Mary Rutledge sat next to her in a fuzzy pink sweater that complemented her round, rosy cheeks. She pushed a plate of chocolate chip cookies in my direction. "Try these. I added pecans instead of walnuts."

A light brown Chihuahua in Mary's lap made herself visible by putting her front paws on the table. Princess, a retired hearing-assistance dog, wore a coat and jeweled collar that matched Mary's top.

"Yah. Good. Crunchy," Ivan Doblinsky, the larger of the two Russian brothers who were part of the group, commented as he finished his cookie.

I expected Elise and Helen might be wondering what was good and crunchy, as I imagined his booming voice had made it down the hallway and into the kitchen.

Ivan's brother, Rudy, and the Professor had their backs to me. They were sorting through piles of black-and-white photos they'd pulled from a cardboard box.

Rudy turned toward me. "Kelly, good to see you."

"Same here," I replied. "What are you working on?"

The Professor glanced over his shoulder. "A while back you gave us some photographs you retrieved from Redwood Heights. We've been so busy we haven't had time to work on them until now."

Mary grinned as she sorted. "Redwood Cove appears to be crime-free at the moment, and we decided to start working on these."

During the restoration of another property owned by Resorts International, I'd found some photos from the eighteen hundreds and had asked the Silver Sentinels if they were interested in sorting them and researching their history. They had been eager to help.

Paper charts on the wall behind them had their names with a list of responsibilities under each. Mary's had *people and clothing*; Gertie's had *mansion, rooms, and stable*. Ivan had the word *logging* under his. Rudy and the Professor had distributed photographs on the sideboard under their names.

"Gertie," the Professor said, "since you're doing the stable, why don't you do carriages, too."

"Good idea." Gertie stood, grabbed her cane, went to the board, and added *carriages* under her name.

It was a good thing her list was on the lower part of the wall or she wouldn't have been able to reach it considering she was only about five feet tall.

She looked at me and explained the process they were using. "We're adding categories as we come across them."

The Professor leaned over and put a photo in Gertie's sort pile.

I walked to the other side of the table and peered around Ivan. His bulk and height didn't make it possible for me to look over him. His photographs showed huge redwood trees in various states of being logged. One showed men sawing and another had teams of mules dragging the felled wood.

I recognized the early owners of the mansion in Mary's stack. The lady of the manor wore a walking suit with lace at the hem and the sleeves. Her hat, tipped slightly to one side of her head, sported a small feather.

"It'll be fun to see what you learn about the history of the place," I said.

"Once we get them sorted, we're going to take some to the museum and meet with the Redwood Cove Historical Society and see what they can tell us," Rudy said.

"Thanks for your help with this," I said.

"We're enjoying it," the Professor said. "Kelly, I recently decided to have a party tomorrow night for Timothy and Clarence—a pie party."

"A pie party? How does that work?"

"Everyone brings a pie and guests get to sample them. It's not necessary for you to bring a pie. There will be plenty. Just bring your charming self. It starts at seven thirty."

"Professor, that doesn't feel right. I want to contribute to the party, too."

"Please, I insist. The inn's kitchen is being used for the class, and you have a full house of guests."

"Okay. I'll agree on one condition. I'll get some ice cream for the party, and I'll make a pie for one of the group's meetings."

"Perfect. Your future pie extends the fun of the pie party," the Professor replied. "I'll send you directions to my home."

I checked the meeting-room schedule on the wall. "There are no meetings scheduled in here for the next few days, so you can leave the photos out."

"Thanks, Kelly," Mary said.

I left them to their project and returned to the work area. Elise had put chopping boards next to some stations and bowls at others. Containers of flour, sugar, and chopped nuts, along with a variety of other ingredients, had been placed on the table. Name cards identified where each person was to sit. Elise had wisely put Ned and Peter at opposite ends of the table.

People began to file in and find their places. They put baskets of collected mushrooms next to their chairs. Ned and Clarence conversed as the remainder of the class got settled. Peter was last. He kept his gaze averted from Ned and Clarence, though I could see a little pink creep up his neck. I was glad he was controlling himself.

Elise stood at the head of the table. "I hope you all had an enjoyable mushroom-hunting experience this afternoon. We won't be using any of the ones you found. The law requires I use only certified mushrooms in my classes because poisonous ones can be hard to identify sometimes. Now it's time to clean, prepare, and cook the ones I've provided. While you're doing that, I'll look at what you've brought in."

She gave instructions to each person as to what they needed to do. Soon knives were chopping, ingredients were being measured, and the cooks were underway. Elise began sorting through the fungi that had been brought in, making notes on a clipboard.

The phone rang.

"Redwood Cove Bed-and-Breakfast," I answered.

"Hello. This is Roger Simmons, and I have a message for Clarence Norton."

"Hi. This is Kelly Jackson. I'd be happy to take the information."

"Please tell him the dog has been approved for the contest. The committee might make changes to the rules in the future, but they feel it's fair for him to use his dog this time."

"I'll let him know. Incidentally, I know you're into woodworking, and I was shown a sinker log today. Fascinating."

"Their grain and coloration are beautiful. I utilized them as much as possible when I built my gallery."

"I'd love to see what they look like."

"I don't have anything scheduled late morning tomorrow. Would you like to come out for a visit then?"

"That'd be perfect."

"How about eleven?"

"I'll be there."

Roger gave me directions, and I hung up. I joined the group at the table. "Clarence, Max has been approved to participate in the hunt Saturday."

"Great." Clarence's habitual laugh punctuated his comment.

I glanced over at Peter. The slight pink had turned crimson. His knife chopped faster and faster. I was glad when the last mushroom on his cutting board disappeared into little pieces and his fingers were still intact.

While the class worked, I helped Helen put out the wine and cheese in the parlor for the guests. An hour later, candy cap mushroom ice cream was beginning to freeze and the aroma of baking cupcakes permeated the air. A smell like maple syrup hung in the air from the candy cap fungi.

Elise finished putting a piece of paper in the last basket. "Thank you for all of your hard work, class. Tomorrow you get to reap the rewards." She put her clipboard down on the table and held up a form. "I've made notes, to the best of my ability, about what type of mushrooms you've found. There's an "eat at your own risk" disclaimer clause at the top of the page. I'm not a licensed mycologist."

Eat at your own risk? That sounded a bit scary.

Elise passed out several papers to the group. "Tomorrow you'll be able to choose from a variety of activities to take you to different mushroom sites in preparation for the contest, which starts Saturday at nine. The awards will be presented Sunday. You meet at the town hall each day. Its location is on the map I gave you. We'll meet back here tomorrow at five for dinner and then feast on the desserts you created today. I wish you all the best of luck in the hunt."

Ned walked over to the counter and sat down, making more notes.

Peter stopped next to him on his way out. "Remember what I said about not following me and not putting any of my information on your website." He uttered the words in a low, menacing voice.

Ned carefully placed his pen next to his notebook. "Your threats mean nothing to me. From what I hear, you're the one who should be worried. There's a logger with a broken nose from a chair you were holding, who plans to get even."

"That's none of your business."

"Maybe there are reasons other than mushrooms behind your concern about being followed." His gaze locked with Peter's. "You know what I'm talking about...the sinker-log wood you've been selling. I checked, and you don't have a permit. There's a lot of grumbling among the locals as to where you're getting it. Most figure you're stealing it. You warned me about people being unhappy. I'm returning the favor."

Peter's fists once again clenched. He put his face next to Ned's. "Like I said, none of your business."

"Everything is my business. I'm a reporter." Ned put his hands on the counter. "I plan on pursuing who is taking the logs. Whoever it is has to have a partner to be able to get them out. If it's you, you and your buddy should be watching over your shoulders."

Peter glared at him, turned, and stomped out. I was relieved nothing more had come of it.

The rest of the class dispersed. I'd noticed the Silver Sentinels leave by the side door so as not to disturb the amateur cooks. I cleared the table as Elise washed pots and pans. Ned continued making notes.

"Time to go." Ned started for the door.

I noticed he'd left his pen. I picked it up and read *Blue Moon Restaurant* on the side. "I'm new to the area. Is this a restaurant I should recommend to people?"

Ned turned and laughed. "No, it's been gone a long time. I imagine the pen is now one of a kind. I like it and its slogan, 'each new day brings a new beginning,' and so I've continued to replace the ink cartridge."

"I understand about finding the right pen. I..."

The sound of banging pots and pans grew so loud, it made it hard to hear. Our conversation stopped.

Ned and I looked at Elise. Her face was contorted and her knuckles white with the intensity with which she gripped the pans.

Ned took a step toward her. "Elise, I'm sorry the restaurant closed."

"Really?" she hissed. "Then why didn't you write an article about the truth of what happened? You only wrote about the food poisoning, which wasn't our fault."

"I didn't know about that until much later. The place was already shut down."

Elise slammed a pot on the counter. "Later could've saved a reputation. Righted a wrong."

"It's over now, Elise. Let it go."

"You can create a reputation or destroy one with every stroke of your pen, with every word you type. You didn't do anything to help the owners or me."

He gathered his things. "Sorry, Elise, it's old history. It happened a long time ago."

She glared at him. "If you were a decent reporter, an honest person, you would let the public know. Telling only part of the truth makes it a lie...and makes you a liar."

"It's too late, Elise."

"It's never too late for someone's reputation."

The words were said to his departing back.

Her gaze bored into him.

If looks could kill...

Chapter 6

Elise turned back to the sink and grabbed the last pot off the counter. I could see a tear roll down her cheek. She brought the back of her hand up in a fast, jerky movement and wiped it away.

"I'm sorry for losing my temper, Kelly." She scrubbed the pan and didn't look at me. "It took months to find the cause of the food poisonings. By then the company responsible was out of business. The owner of the restaurant, a friend of mine, ended up having a stroke. A dark cloud hung over my head from people wondering if it was my fault. I had a hard time getting work."

"It sounds like you have every reason to be upset."

She glanced at me and blinked a few times. "Thanks. The restaurant business is tough as it is. Places come and go. Unexpected problems only make it worse." She sighed. "But I love the work. That's why I stay with it."

"Loving what you do for a living is a wonderful experience that some people never have. Some don't even know what would bring them that feeling. Being able to love what you do is special, and you've had the strength to stick with it, even when it's been difficult. It shows your depth of passion."

Elise stopped what she was doing and looked at me. "I really like what you just said. I've never thought of it in quite that way." She finished drying the pot and put it away. "Thanks."

The sound of crunching gravel outside, the inn's unplanned doorbell, announced the arrival of a vehicle. We both looked out the window of the back door. A red monster truck covered in dirt and riding high on oversize tires pulled in. I'd noticed many of Redwood Cove's young adults favored this type of vehicle.

"That's my son," Elise said. "He's bringing food for the dinner."

The buzzer on the oven went off. "The cupcakes are done." She began pulling out trays and putting them on cooling racks.

"I'll go out and show him where the refrigerators are in the storage shed."

"I appreciate it. I'll straighten the room and get my equipment packed up. By then these should be cool, and I can put them away and get out of your hair."

"Don't worry. You're not in the way."

While we'd been talking, Helen had been coming into the kitchen every so often to replenish trays. Since she'd prepared the food earlier, everything went quickly and smoothly for the guests' evening appetizers.

I went out the door and down the steps. A thin-faced young man in blue jeans with a long blond ponytail clambered down from his high perch.

I smiled. "Hi. I'm Kelly Jackson. Your mom's finishing up inside. She said you have supplies. I'll show you where they go."

"I'm Joey. Pleased to meet you."

An enormous winch on the front of his pickup caught my eye. "We have one of those on a truck at our ranch in Wyoming. It's not anywhere near as big as yours, though."

"My friends and I do a lot of off-roading. It's come in handy a number of times when we've gotten stuck." He opened the truck's tailgate and took out a box.

"I bet it has." I saw a paper bag in the back of the pickup. "Is that part of the food for tomorrow?"

"Yep. Everything in there is for Mom."

I picked it up and gestured for him to follow. In the shed, I flipped on the light and led the way to two double-door stainless steel refrigerators.

"The one on the left has a lot of room in it," I said. "We'll use that one first and see if everything fits."

With two of us unloading, we were done in less than ten minutes. Joey and I went to the work area.

"Hi, Mom." He gave Elise a quick hug. "I was able to get everything on your list, and it's all put away."

"Thanks. I appreciate your help."

"A couple of my friends and I want to go out driving for about an hour. I got some new spotlights for the truck at a garage sale and want to try them out. Then we're going to have burgers at O'Toole's Sports Bar."

"You boys have a good time, and I'll see you when you get home."

"Don't wait up for me. I might stay and watch a basketball game."

"Okay."

Joey said good-bye and left. Elise had stored the cupcakes in plastic containers. Helen came in with a tray of dirty dishes and glasses. A familiar rattling in the driveway told me Daniel had arrived. A few minutes later, the back door burst open, and Tommy, Helen's son, ran into the room, followed by Allie, a slender girl with ebony hair to her waist. Her dad didn't follow her in, so she closed the door behind her.

Tommy slid to a halt when he saw Elise, appearing startled at the sight of an unfamiliar person in the kitchen.

At the same time, a distant howling began. It came from the direction of Helen's cottage. I realized Fred, Tommy's basset hound, was nowhere to be seen, but it was clear he knew Tommy was home. The baying became louder and louder and continued at full volume on the back porch. Daniel's face appeared in the window, and he opened the door.

Tommy threw himself down on his knees, flung his arms wide, and called, "Fred!"

The dog was all motion—ears flapping, legs pumping, and tail wagging. The short-legged, long-bodied tricolored dog hurtled into Tommy's chest. Boy and dog rolled over and over, Tommy laughing, Fred crooning.

"Okay, you two. Enough." Helen shook her head and smiled. "Tommy, this is Elise Jenkins. She's teaching the mushroom class I told you about." Helen looked at Elise. "My son, Tommy, and his four-legged sidekick, Fred."

"Hi," Tommy said.

Fred gave her a basset-hound grin and a tail wave.

Daniel put his hand on Allie's shoulder. "This is my daughter, Allie."

"Nice to meet you," Allie said.

"Same here," Elise replied.

Daniel sat at the counter. "I only saw Elise's car in the lot and when I peeked through the window I could see the class was over. I thought it would be okay to free Fred."

Helen nodded. "I'm glad you did, and I suspect you made our neighbors happy as well with all the noise he was making."

Tommy jumped to his feet and noticed the fungi on the table and began pointing. "Pig's ear. Chanterelle. Puff ball. Or it could be a poisonous amanita."

Allie joined him. "There's a hedgehog and a pink coral mushroom."

Elise went over to the table. "I'm impressed you both know so much about mushrooms. They aren't something I've had many kids show an interest in."

Allie spoke up. "The school starts teaching us about mushrooms in first grade. They want us to know that some are very dangerous so we can be careful and also watch out for our animals. There's a unit every year at each grade level teaching us different information about them."

Tommy dropped down on the floor next to Fred and hugged him around his neck. "They have lessons about them in art, science, math, reading, and writing. What you get taught depends on how old you are. It's cool."

Elise picked up her toolbox of kitchen equipment. "I'm glad to know that. It's nice the school system is teaching you about the area you live in." She looked at me. "I'll be back tomorrow at three to set up for the dinner."

"I'm looking forward to it," I said. "*Even* the mushroom cupcakes. They smelled divine this afternoon."

"It should be fun." Elise waved from the door. "Bye."

Allie and Daniel left. Tommy settled in a beanbag chair, with Fred draped over his lap, and turned on the television. Helen checked on the appetizers and then pulled out the baskets we'd use to deliver breakfast to the guests tomorrow. We had settled into a comfortable routine.

"I'm going to work on some files," I said. "I'll take care of the fire, like we discussed. You don't need to come back after dinner."

"And I'll be over earlier in the morning to get the coffee and tea ready."

We were creating a good team. I'd taken over tending the fire in the evening to give Tommy and Helen more time together. We'd had guests requesting drinks be available earlier in the morning, so she was handling that.

I went back to my rooms and grabbed leftovers from my refrigerator. After heating them in the microwave, I sat down to look at some orders.

The cell phone rang. The number showed it was Scott Thompson, an administrator for the same company I worked for. My heart was like a dysfunctional team of horses—one wanted to leap for joy, the other kick and run away.

My marriage had ended abruptly, due to my once best friend and my husband deciding they wanted to be together, and the experience had left me relationship leery. Baby steps were all I was willing to take.

Scott had recently agreed to create a center to improve the lives of local residents in a variety of ways including classes on nutrition and opportunities for organic gardening. There was even a herd of llamas to provide wool for weaving. It was a project dear to the heart of our boss, Michael Corrigan. He loved the community and wanted to do something special for the people of the town.

"Hi, Scott. Nice to hear from you. How are you doing?"

"Fine. Redwood Cove Community Center is beginning to come together, and I've had time to settle in and start trying some new recipes."

I remember how surprised I was when I discovered he was a gourmet cook. His position in the company had him on the road most of the time. The offer he'd accepted would keep him in Redwood Cove for at least two months, a big change of pace for him.

"I'm glad to hear it. I know that's something you wanted to pursue during your stay here."

"Do you like guinea pigs?"

What in the world?

"Why…why do you ask? You know how much I love animals. Do you…do you have one you need to find a home for?"

"No. I'm wondering if you'd be willing to be one and come over for dinner tomorrow at five thirty."

I laughed. "I'd love to, as long as I don't have to dress up like a guinea pig."

"Great! See you then."

We said our good-byes and I checked the parlor. It was empty. I closed the doors on the fireplace, checked the locks on all the doors, and called it a night.

* * * *

The next morning I'd finished picking up the last breakfast basket when Daniel arrived. He entered with a large box of produce in his arms. I unpacked it while he went back to his vehicle for more food. Helen had gone to wake up Tommy. We'd finished putting everything away when a deputy sheriff's car pulled in beside the blue bus.

A figure I knew well emerged from the vehicle—Deputy Sheriff Bill Stanton. I wondered what brought him here. He'd been helping Tommy with a science project, but I didn't think that was it because he was in uniform. He occasionally took his breakfast break here. Helen prepared it for him as a thank-you, but she wasn't fixing anything now.

I'd know soon.

He knocked at the back door, and I waved him in.

"Good morning, Deputy Stanton. How are you?"

He gave a rueful smile. "Already tired. A very early start this morning. Doesn't bode well for the long day ahead."

"Sounds like coffee time. Have a seat at the counter, and I'll bring you some."

He pulled a stool out and settled his large frame onto it. "I'd sure appreciate it."

I knew he took it black from previous visits. I poured him a large mug, handed it to him, and sat down next to him with my own cup in hand. "What brings you here?"

Daniel had joined us and was leaning on the counter.

Deputy Stanton took a sip of the dark liquid, then put the cup down and looked at me. "Found your name in a notebook and a date for a meeting."

I wonder what this is about.

"Whose notebook?"

"Ned Blaine's." The officer put his hands around the mug. "He's been murdered."

Chapter 7

I put my coffee cup down with a loud thud. "Oh, my gosh! What happened?"

"That's what we're trying to piece together. He was found shot to death this morning. We figured it happened last night. We'll know more about the time after the autopsy report. Right now we're working on when he was last seen."

Deputy Stanton looked at Daniel. "I'm glad you're here. You were on my list of people to talk to. He was found on your tribe's sacred ground in Mallory National Park."

I sat up straighter. "Daniel and I were there yesterday afternoon picking mushrooms. Ned was here when I got back. He was taking the mushroom class taught by Elise Jenkins."

"What time did you last see him?" Stanton had his pen and pad out.

"About six."

"Did he say anything about where he was going?"

I shook my head. "No."

The deputy turned to Daniel. "Did you see him yesterday?"

"No. I dropped Kelly off and went to pick up Tommy and Allie."

"Was yesterday afternoon the last time either of you visited the site?"

"It was for me," I said. "I was here the rest of the night."

"Actually, I did go to the park again," Daniel said. "A friend of mine knew I was planning to mushroom hunt there. He called and left a message asking me to get some chanterelles for him. I heard it when I returned home. The kids were busy with their homework, and I knew where there were a lot of them since I'd just been there. I took a quick trip to the site."

"Did you see Ned or anyone else?"

"No. I went out and back."

"Kelly, in any of the conversations you had with Ned or what you observed during the class, did you hear or see anything that made you think someone might want to harm him or had a serious problem with him?"

I thought of Elise and the issues she faced. I hated to involve her, but there was no way I could dodge such a direct question and be honest.

I sighed and recounted the altercations between Peter and Ned and the conversation with Elise. I remembered Elise's wish-you-were-dead look to Ned's departing back but didn't mention it. That was my interpretation, and she didn't need any more grief in her life right now.

Stanton sipped his coffee. "He was a reporter. That meant stepping on toes now and then, and he never hesitated or backed off when he was on a story. I heard about the mushroom-site book he was writing and how he was selling information over the Internet. Not illegal, but people were upset."

"How much are the mushrooms worth?" I asked.

"Depends on the type, condition, and availability. The right time and place, and a serious fungi hunter can bring in thousands of dollars in a day."

Stunned, I said, "I had no idea. That sounds like enough money that someone would kill to keep their areas secret."

"You bet," Stanton said.

Daniel pulled a stool out and sat at the counter with us.

Stanton eyed him. "Daniel, tell me what Ned was up to that involved you. I saw your name and notes from a talk the two of you had. Haven't had time to read them yet."

"Ned questioned my tribe's right to claim the knoll at Carson River as a sacred site. It gives us privileges in terms of using the land that others don't have. Ned didn't think it was fair, and he pushed for proof of our assertions."

"How did your people get it designated as sacred?"

"Ceremonies have been performed there for generations. We know because it's part of the history told in stories passed down through the years. The area has spiritual significance to us. Ned wanted something more concrete."

"Were you able to provide him with anything?"

"There were ceremonial items found there, but he claimed they could've been planted. His words angered some of the younger men. The rest of us let it roll off our backs. Ned didn't have any power. We decided we'd deal with it if we ever had to. The Feds are the ones in charge, and we weren't struck by Ned having an inside track there."

"Can you give me the names of those who were upset?"

"Sure, Deputy Stanton. I'll write them down for you. While some of them were mad, I think you have much better suspects who are linked to his news reporting and his mushroom-area quest. He was just at the digging stage with us. Nothing threatened the site's status."

Stanton closed his notepad. "Makes sense, but I have to gather all the information I can."

"I understand," Daniel said.

Stanton stood and stretched. "Gotta go. Thanks for the coffee."

"You're welcome. I hope you can find out who did this as soon as possible," I said.

Deputy Stanton nodded. "So do I."

Crunching gravel announced the arrival of another visitor. Through the back window I saw Elise park her vehicle next to the police car and then emerge carrying a box. Joey's monster truck drove in and stopped next to his mother's sedan.

I opened the back door for her. "Good morning, Elise."

"Hi, Kelly." She entered and put the box on the counter. "I made a mushroom-carrot-cheese loaf for you and one for Helen as a thank-you for letting me take over the kitchen."

"That's really nice of you."

"Joey's bringing in some additional food for tonight." Elise glanced at Deputy Stanton, a questioning look on her face. "Hello, Deputy Stanton."

The officer took a step toward Elise and pulled out his notepad. "Morning, Elise. I need to ask you a few questions."

She frowned. "What's this about?"

"Ned Blaine was murdered last night. I know you had some hard feelings toward him when the restaurant closed."

Her eyes widened a fraction and her face drained of color.

Stanton took out a pen. "Where were you last night?"

"Home alone baking and watching television," she replied in a defiant tone, her jaw now set in a firm line.

Joey had gotten out of his truck and was coming up the back steps with a paper bag. I opened the door for him.

Elise took the bag and put it next to the food she'd brought. "And in case you were wondering what my son was doing last night, he had a bite to eat with his friends and then watched a basketball game." She looked at Joey. "Isn't that right?"

"Yeah. Why?"

"Blaine got himself killed last night," she said. "The deputy here is checking on where people were."

"We're asking that you make your decisions for tomorrow by five today so the vendors know how many to prepare for. There will be a box on the table for you to put your forms in."

Members of the different businesses gave five-minute overviews of what they offered and half an hour was designated for people to ask questions and sign up for what they wanted to do.

When that was finished, Roger addressed the crowd. "You've now had an opportunity to learn about your choices and make your decisions as to what you're doing today. We're out to see who can find the widest variety of mushrooms tomorrow. There are two groups—locals who live within thirty miles of town and are familiar with the area, and people outside of that. The winners will receive a carved redwood mushroom with a winner's plaque. No prize money is involved. It's just for fun. This is a good faith contest and we're trusting you to follow the rule about not picking mushrooms today."

People nodded in agreement.

"You've been given permission to go on some private property. I want you to know the owners have surveillance cameras at some sites where rare mushrooms are found because of their monetary worth. You have permits for the parks and some of their areas are monitored as well. Anyone seen picking mushrooms on the cameras today will automatically be disqualified. Now, if you'll…"

A loud squeal followed by a series of grunts disrupted his final words. I saw a tall, lean man walking a black-and-white potbellied pig in a harness down a ramp attached to a pickup truck. The pig squealed again when it reached the ground. Her curly tail never stopped moving.

I realized Peter had moved next to me during Roger's speech.

His face flushed red. "What the…"

Roger cleared his throat. "We have some unusual participants this year in the form of two animals trained to find mushrooms. We have a dog, Maximillian, and a pig named Priscilla. The committee hasn't had requests to use animals before. It's being allowed this year. After the contest is over, they will meet and discuss what the rules are in the future."

Peter began slamming his right fist into his left hand. A loud smacking sound punctuated each hit. I spied Deputy Stanton in the crowd near us. He walked in our direction.

Stanton stopped in front of Peter. "Quite the temper you have there. That's what led to the incident at the bar a few nights ago."

Peter glared at him, his lips clamped shut.

Stanton continued, "I hear you've had problems with Ned Blaine. When was the last time you talked to him?"

"Yesterday afternoon at the mushroom class. Why do you want to know?" Peter asked in a challenging tone.

"What were you doing last night?" Deputy Stanton asked.

"I was home watching television until I went to bed." Peter's nostrils flared. "Like I said, why do you want to know?"

"Can anyone verify that?"

"No. I was alone. Stanton, what is this about?"

"Are you sure yesterday afternoon was the last time you saw Ned Blaine? Or did you see him last night and your temper got out of control? Did you lose it and kill him?"

Chapter 8

Brash, hotheaded Peter stepped back from the deputy. He began shaking his head. "No way. No way you're going to pin this on me." Peter took another step back. "I didn't like the guy, but I didn't kill him. He had plenty of enemies."

"I'm not accusing you, Peter." Stanton smiled, but it didn't reach his eyes. "Just asking questions."

"Anything else, Deputy Stanton?" Peter spat the words out.

"Not for now."

Peter stamped off without a good-bye or a backward look.

Stanton looked at me. "Thanks again for the coffee." With a nod, he left.

Roger was no longer at the podium. I'd been so engrossed in the exchange between the officer and Peter, I hadn't heard his final comments. The Professor, Timothy, and Clarence had joined the man with Priscilla the pig. I walked over to them.

I stopped next to the Professor. "Were any more instructions given? I didn't hear the last part of what was said."

"Roger said the activities would begin in half an hour and there was still time to sign up."

"What are you going to do first?"

"I'm not going. I'll stay here and enjoy a cup of coffee. Timothy and Clarence plan to hike. Priscilla and her owner are going to go along with them."

"It should be fun seeing the dog and pig hunting mushrooms."

The Professor nodded. "I agree. They are bike riding after that. Then this afternoon the boys are doing horseback riding, canoeing, and off-roading, in that order."

"Thanks for telling me. I'll go register."

I went to the appropriate table and filled out the form, leaving the morning clear after hiking. I ran into Roger on my way back.

"Are we still on for later this morning?" he asked.

"Yes. I'm looking forward to seeing the sinker wood."

Roger raised an eyebrow. "Tell me again how you learned about sinker logs."

I explained about my mushroom hunt with Daniel and the tree he'd pointed out to me in the river.

"I know the one you're talking about. It's a beaut. I filed for a permit to get it but had no luck. It'll stay where it is."

"Why wouldn't they let you take it?"

"It's an environmental issue. The Park Service is worried about altering the stream bed."

"I see. Sorry it didn't work out for you."

"There are still opportunities for me to buy that type of wood. People have logs stashed away."

The volunteer I'd seen earlier tapped on the mic. "Attention, everyone. The events will start in ten minutes."

"I'll tell you more about it when we meet." Roger went to the podium.

I joined the men, the dog, and the pig. Constant motion described Priscilla—ears bouncing, tail flapping, feet moving. Her perpetual grin made me want to grin back. A large pink bow had been put on her collar.

"May I pet her?" I asked the owner.

"You bet. She loves that."

Her wiry, coarse black-and-white hair felt like thin wires. She snorted with pleasure as I scratched behind her ears.

"I have a mushroom-hunting pig at home. How did you train her?" Clarence asked. "By the way, I'm Clarence Norton."

"Ted Pearson. Glad to meet you. Ah, man, she's a natural at truffles. I hardly had to do a thing."

They launched into the details of fungi pig-training as I patted the top of Priscilla's head.

Roger's voice interrupted them. "It's time for the mushroom hunting practice to begin. I hope you all have a lot of fun today."

"Thanks for letting me pet her, Ted. I'm Kelly Jackson."

"Anytime," he replied.

We walked over to where we'd registered and received instructions and maps. The place we'd be hiking was close to town, but not within walking distance. We split up to get our vehicles so we could gather at the site in half an hour.

When I arrived at the park, everyone was already there. Priscilla once again walked down her ramp, making pig noises. Max bounded around her, occasionally going into play pose, trying to entice her to engage. She wasn't interested.

"Sorry, Max. Priscilla knows it's hunt time. She's all business now," Ted said.

Our leader, a short man with bushy blond hair and a healthy-sized beard, told us we'd walk a short distance together, then he'd show us different areas on the map where we might find fungi.

A cacophony of sound echoed through the normally tranquil forest as Priscilla trotted along grunting, squealing, and snorting. Max punctuated her commentary every so often with loud barks. Priscilla's hooves made an even beat as she bounced down the trail. She seemed to barely touch the ground.

I turned to her owner. "It's like she's tap dancing."

"I call her Miss Twinkle Toes at times."

We came to a split in the trail and the guide showed us where it was on our maps and how to get to areas marked for mushrooms.

"We'll meet back at the vehicles in half an hour. I'll stay here to answer any questions you might have."

Clarence, Timothy, and Ted decided which directions they'd go, so that each of them would have privacy on their hunt. I wanted to watch the pig in action. I figured I'd have a chance to see Max on the job later in the day.

"May I join you?" I asked Priscilla's owner. "I'd love to see her work, and I'm not entered in the contest."

"Sure. She loves an audience. Just don't try to take a mushroom away from her. She's never hurt anyone…yet…but I know people who have shorter fingers after reaching for a mushroom their pig wanted."

"No worries there," I said.

Priscilla immediately began scurrying from spot to spot, rooting with her nose. The dank smell of moist soil and disturbed, molding leaves filled the air. Her owner carried a small, shallow-tined rake.

"Pigs love truffles. They don't really need much in the way of training to find those. Truffles are underground and the pigs can smell them. Just have to be fast with the rake or they'll eat them. Those are what I'm more interested in finding today. They're worth a lot of money."

Priscilla dug energetically with her snout at a particularly interesting spot. Her owner threw some food a short distance from it, and she turned and gobbled it up. He raked the area and pulled out a dirt-covered fungus.

"Bingo! A truffle!" He put it in his basket. "I checked with the contest committee, and they said it was okay for me to pick any I found today. Mushrooms and truffles are related, but there's an ongoing argument about whether or not a truffle is a mushroom because of the many differences between them, the main one being they are found underground."

We continued our search with Priscilla in the lead.

"I went a step further and taught her to find regular 'shrooms like dogs do."

"How do you train animals to find them?"

"You get vials of scent, hide it different places, and reward them when they find it. Start easy, in a place inside a yard, and work your way outside to unfamiliar places. They catch on fast. I can see most of the mushrooms, but she finds the ones covered in leaves."

Priscilla grunted and rooted into the ground, creating troughs with her snout. She would stop at above-ground mushrooms and look at her owner for a treat. He tossed her one, and we moved on. The time passed quickly.

When we returned to the parking lot, I said, "Thank you so much for letting me tag along. That was fascinating."

He scratched the top of Priscilla's head. "She's a good ol' pig. We're a good team."

We returned to our vehicles, then rendezvoused back at the town hall. The next event was scheduled to begin in half an hour.

"We're riding bicycles next," Clarence volunteered. "Max will have to miss out on this one. He'll stay in the truck. It's in the shade, windows are open, and, with the cool ocean breeze, he'll be fine. Are you going to join us, Kelly?"

"No. Roger Simmons invited me to his gallery to learn more about redwood trees in general and sinker logs in particular."

The Professor rejoined the group as I said this. "I visited his studio on one of his open house days. He's a very talented woodworker, and he's collected some outstanding pieces of redwood."

I bid them farewell and headed for the truck I'd parked on the street. Daniel's bus pulled in behind it as I approached.

Deputy Sheriff Stanton drove in behind him.

Now what?

Daniel's tall, lanky form emerged, and he glanced in the deputy's direction. A slight frown creased his forehead. Stanton hadn't gotten out yet.

He waited for me at my vehicle. "Hi, Kelly. What did you do for your first activity?"

"I went hiking with Priscilla the pig."

We shared a laugh, then stopped as Deputy Stanton slammed his car door. He walked over to us, Ned's notebook in his hand.

"Daniel, I have some more questions for you. Let's step over to my car."

Daniel didn't move. "As far as I'm concerned, there's nothing we have to talk about that Kelly can't hear. I have nothing to hide, and we work together."

"Okay. Your choice." He flipped open the notebook to a bookmark. "It seems there was something you didn't tell me earlier." He ran his finger down the page and stopped. "Says here you threatened Ned Blaine."

Chapter 9

Daniel stiffened, then became still, except for a twitch in his left cheek.

"It appears it had something to do with your daughter, Allie. Tell me about it."

"Ned questioned her one day when she was on her way home from school. Wanted her to talk to him about why our site got designated as sacred. When she tried to walk away, Ned grabbed her arm. He scared her. I found out and then I found him. I told him not to touch Allie or talk to her ever again."

Ned accosted Allie. Not a good thing.

"How did he react?"

"He apologized. Said he'd stepped over the bounds of what was acceptable. Promised he wouldn't approach her again. Ned kept his word."

"Any other interactions with him?"

"Just the times he questioned me and the others about the site."

Deputy Stanton closed the notebook. "Where were you last night?"

"Home with my daughter."

"Can anyone else corroborate that?"

Daniel's rigid shoulders indicated he hadn't lost any of his tenseness. "No."

"You know, Daniel…people would understand if you felt your daughter was threatened and you protected her."

"Like I said, Deputy Stanton, that was the end of it where Allie was concerned."

"Okay. Remember, if you hear anything, let me know."

"I will."

Stanton left and Daniel and I stared at each other. His face looked like chiseled stone. My stomach churned.

"Whew! Daniel, I'm not sure he believed you."

"Me neither, but what I told him is the truth."

I cleared my throat. "I certainly believe you. But…you have no alibi, and you went back to the site."

Daniel shoved his hands into the pockets of his blue jeans. "I didn't do anything, so they won't find anything."

"I've read about people being arrested even when they weren't guilty."

"I've read that, too. But there's nothing I can do except keep telling the truth."

Daniel could be in serious trouble. What could I do to help? Then I had it.

"There *is* something *we* can do. We can work on finding out who killed Ned. And we have a whole team who can help with that. The Silver Sentinels."

Daniel nodded. "I like the idea of taking action. I'll meet with the elders of our tribe to see if they think someone they know might have killed Ned."

"I'll get in touch with the Silver Sentinels. I'll keep you informed about any plans we make."

"Thanks, Kelly. It's nice to know I have you in my corner."

"You bet. Besides, if something happened to you, who would bring us our pizza on a regular basis or make your famous triple hot chocolate?"

He grinned and his face softened. His shoulders dropped into a more relaxed position.

Daniel drove off, and I went to find the Professor. I caught sight of him standing with Clarence and Timothy. I wanted to keep Daniel's involvement private so decided I'd wait to talk with him until after the others had left.

I noticed white bike helmets on the two friends. "Looks like you're ready for your next event."

"Yes. Max is safely tucked away. He can rest up for the canoe ride." Clarence looked at his watch. "Time to go."

They walked over to where a trailer held a row of bikes, leaving me alone with the Professor.

"Professor, I need to talk with you."

I shared what had just taken place. "I have an appointment with Roger Simmons, but I can meet with everyone at lunchtime if they're available."

He already had his phone out. "I'll check on that and let you know."

The Sentinels had a very effective phone tree. I'd know soon if they could meet.

I walked across the grassy field to my vehicle. I unlocked the pickup, got in, and put on my seat belt. Before I could start the engine, I heard a familiar ping. I checked my phone.

Soon was right.

They'd all be at the conference room at noon and would bring lunch. I called Helen, told her what was happening, and asked her to make the room ready, then texted Daniel.

I drove along the coast, the bright blue Pacific Ocean on my right. The waves varied in intensity. When a strong one hit the rocky shoreline, water exploded high into the air. The rise and fall of the swell, like a creature breathing, made the ocean a living body. Having grown up in Wyoming, the dramatic scene continued to delight me.

I passed the Red Carriage Inn. Roger told me I'd see a wrought iron gate a short way past it and he'd leave it open for me. I spied it and pulled onto the paved driveway. I stopped and studied the structure. A metal redwood tree adorned the front and was probably about seven feet tall. Several iron deer appeared to graze next to it on the right. On the other side, several small redwoods had a bird soaring over them. There was a surprising amount of detail from feathers on the bird to grooves on the antlers. Clearly a skilled metalworker had created the gate.

Continuing on, I drove uphill, out onto a grassy flat area, and parked. The studio's floor-to-ceiling glass windows looked out onto a stunning view of the Pacific Ocean. I could understand why Roger wanted this place. The driveway continued on and up to a large sprawling home. The gallery occupied what had been the restaurant where Elise had worked. A connected barnlike structure loomed over the back of it. Roger appeared at the door to the studio and waved to me.

I got out and waved back. "Hi. You have a gorgeous view."

"It's one I never tire of, and I feel its beauty and the constant motion help the artist within me to create." He smiled. "Come on in and let me show you around."

Lifelike wooden creatures greeted me as I stepped into the gallery. Flying birds hung from the ceiling, and a deer on a pedestal gazed at me from a corner of the room. A miniature whale swam next to one of the windows, with the ocean in the background.

These weren't the rough-hewn bears I'd seen for sale outside of tourist stores. The polished wood gleamed, and the smooth, rounded contours of the animals reflected the room's lights. While I didn't know much about woodworking, to achieve that sheen must have meant hours of sanding and polishing.

"Roger, these are incredible. It's not just the sculptures, but there's a connection I feel with the animals. It's like they're looking at me. You've caught that perfectly."

"Thanks. As an artist, it's always a pleasure when someone has an affinity for your work." He picked up two redwood mushrooms on a table near the front door. "These are the prizes for the mushroom-hunting part of the contest."

I admired the grains running through the shining mushroom caps. They had brass winner's plaques attached to their bases. I put them down.

"Your gate is amazing as well."

"I designed it, and a local artist made it. I wanted something that reflected the area."

"I'd say it definitely does."

He ushered me around, pointing out different pieces. The multicolored grain of the wood was like nothing I'd ever seen. Blues and greens intertwined with the expected red and brown tones.

I examined an inquisitive sea lion with a tilted head. "The colors are amazing."

"They're caused by minerals in the water where the logs rested for many years." He ran his hand down the arched back of the marine mammal. "That's why the wood is so valuable. It's from logging in the eighteen hundreds, and what there is of it is all anyone is ever going to get."

"Are you still able to buy it?"

"Yes, but it's when a seller decides to let go of some of it. There are stashes of the wood here and there. People dole them out when they need money. The longer they hold on to them, the more valuable they become. Luckily, people usually come to me first because they know I'll pay top dollar...although I have lost out to Asian buyers on a few occasions."

"Thank you for showing me your collection."

"Let me show you my work area. You said you wanted to know more about the process."

"I do."

He opened a door at the back wall marked PRIVATE. I entered a structure that reminded me of our barns at home, with its high ceiling and expansive area. A forklift similar to one on the ranch occupied a corner. Tables and freestanding saws were scattered around the room. Rows of equipment I didn't recognize hung on the wall. Roger started to tell me about everything.

A half hour later I knew what a fish-tail carving tool looked like and why it had an octagonal handle—easier to grip and it wouldn't roll when put down. My vocabulary now included "flexible shaft power grinder" as well.

"Thank you for the fascinating and informative tour. I love learning about something new. There are so many micro worlds for people to participate in."

We walked over to a pile of lumber.

Roger pointed to it. "These are dried sinker logs. It takes about two years to get the moisture out, and they need to be cut a certain way to dry properly."

I noticed two damp logs suspended on chains. "What are those?"

"Those are fresh sinker logs I recently bought. They'll have to go through the curing process. I'll have them moved to another property I own."

Remembering Daniel's comments, I asked, "So, were those people able to get permits?"

"There are still a few logs in the water on private land, and they don't need permits. They rarely become available. These came from Peter, the guy in the mushroom class, and Elise's son helped deliver them. Peter said they came from property he'd recently inherited. I didn't question him. Someone was going to buy them, so I figured it might as well be me."

I wondered if he knew anything about Ned Blaine's suspicions.

"Did you know one of the town's reporters, Ned Blaine, has been murdered?"

"Yes. Something like that gets around the community quickly."

"He'd questioned Peter about sinker logs. Implied he might be getting them illegally."

"Like I said, I don't know, didn't ask. Peter also brings me dried wood, so he has access to some that's been around for a while."

How far could I push the questioning? "How well did you know Ned Blaine?"

A frown creased Roger's forehead. "Not well. He wrote a flattering article about the studio and my work. Why do you ask?"

"Sorry. Just curiosity, I guess. I was talking to this man yesterday afternoon and now he's dead. It's unnerving."

Roger's brow cleared. "I understand. Sometimes it helps to talk about experiences like that."

"I need to get back to the inn. Thank you again for the tour."

"Happy to do it."

He walked me to my car, and we said good-bye.

As I pulled onto the highway, I thought about what I had learned. Peter was involved with retrieving fresh sinker logs as Ned had implied, but he claimed they were legal. Elise's son, Joey, worked with him. Roger bought as much as he could and most people went to him when they wanted to sell. He didn't question where they came from.

I didn't know if any of this would prove helpful for Daniel, but it was a start. I felt he was more worried than he was letting on. Being involved in a murder investigation would feel uncomfortable under any circumstances. With the murdered man writing that Daniel had threatened him, even more so.

Chapter 10

I entered the conference room and found Mary, Gertie, and the Professor whisking photos off their work area and into labeled boxes. Helen had placed glasses, dishes, utensils, and napkins on the sideboard, as well as water and coffee.

Ivan entered with a red padded container slung over his shoulder. He put it on a chair, unzipped the top, and pulled out a large plastic container, which he placed on the table. Rudy followed him in with a small ice chest.

Gertie removed the lid from the container and pulled out a platter of sandwiches cut into quarters. "Thanks for carrying the food, Ivan."

"I like to help. Carrying is something I can do."

"And do well," Gertie added.

Muscle made up much of Ivan's bulk. He routinely worked on *Nadia*, his high-maintenance fishing boat, scrubbing and painting. His daily walks with his brother added to his fitness.

You wouldn't know they were brothers. Rudy's neatly trimmed beard and mustache contrasted sharply with the thick, bushy hair covering Ivan's upper lip. The older brother's bulk emphasized Rudy's slight build. The only time I heard Rudy's Russian accent was when he was excited or upset.

Rudy took a bowl from the ice chest and removed the cover. Bright yellow chunks of pineapple mingled with red and green grapes and vivid red cherries.

"Thanks, everyone, for being willing to meet on such short notice," I said. "I'm concerned about Daniel."

The Professor pulled notepads and pens from a drawer and placed them in front of where people would be sitting. "As are we, my dear. Being interrogated in a murder investigation is a serious matter."

Mary nodded. "We know he's innocent and wouldn't kill someone, but mistakes are made and innocent people have gone to prison."

She echoed the concern I had voiced.

Rudy put a serving spoon in the fruit bowl. "The Professor told us about the questioning. Parents are protective of their children. People could easily see Daniel doing whatever he felt necessary to protect his daughter…and feel he had a right to do so."

"Let's fill our plates and get down to business," Gertie said. "Kelly, the choices are chicken, tuna salad, and vegetarian. We went through our cupboards and refrigerators, met at my house, and put together lunch with what we had."

I placed one of each on my plate. "They look delicious."

Gertie picked up a bag on a chair next to her and handed it to me. "Luckily I baked my favorite Pennsylvania Dutch wheat berry bread yesterday, so we had plenty of that. I brought half of a loaf for you."

"Thanks! Homemade bread has a flavor all its own." I put the loaf on a tray resting on the sideboard.

I took a bite of the tuna sandwich. The bread's crunchiness went well with the smooth texture of the salad. The vegetarian consisted of cream cheese, tomatoes, cucumbers, and sprouts.

"The chicken is the smoked organic the market has just started carrying," the Professor said.

Everyone filled their plates and got settled.

"Here's dessert." Mary added a container of oversize chocolate chip cookies to the impromptu feast. The cookies' sweet scent drifted over to me.

She reached over to the chair next to her and unzipped her dog purse. Princess popped into view. Her pink coat matched Mary's pink sweater. The rose-colored jewels of her collar sparkled in the room's light.

The Professor stood and retrieved the chart stand from the corner. He placed it next to the table. "Our goal is to find out who killed Ned Blaine and do it as fast as possible."

"Did any of you know him?" I asked.

The Professor chose a Magic Marker from the drawer. "I don't believe any of us knew him as a personal friend."

The group members affirmed this statement with comments and nods.

Gertie put a couple of spoonfuls of fruit salad on her plate. "Ned interviewed us each time we were involved in a case. He was quite pleasant and very complimentary in what he wrote."

Mary nodded. "He was the main reporter for the paper, so he covered just about everything that went on, from the church bazaar and school fund-raisers to theft and murder. His articles were very thorough."

"He followed the criminal cases and, being a reporter, he also did investigative work, finding out things people didn't want to come to light," Rudy said. "He could have a lot of enemies. Where do we begin?"

"I know three areas he was working on," I volunteered. "Mushroom-hunting areas, sinker logs, and the Native American sacred classification of the area near the Carson River."

"Let's start a chart for each of those," Gertie suggested.

The Professor did as requested and taped them on the wall.

"When I heard he was killed," I said, "I wondered what emotions drive people to murder. What do you think some of those would be?"

The group chimed in, calling out the words *fear, jealousy, hatred, greed*, and *revenge*. Ivan's booming voice added *anger*.

The Professor added those to a fourth chart. "Now let's think about which of these might be behind his death. Let's prioritize them as best we can where Ned was concerned."

Mary stared at the list. "I think jealousy, wanting what someone else has, is the least likely. He was a modest man, lived in a small home, and drove an older compact car. I've seen him around town frequently, but never with someone."

Rudy leaned forward. "I'd put anger as number one. It's a heated emotion and causes people to react in ways they might not normally do, and the work he did pushed a lot of buttons."

Gertie nodded. "Also, anger can spill over into the other areas. Fear can trigger anger and hatred. Revenge is another form of anger."

The Professor made a second list on the chart paper with *anger* underlined at the top and *fear, hatred*, and *revenge* underneath it. *Jealousy* went to the bottom of the page, while *greed* occupied the middle.

"Let's look at the areas where he was working and list the names of people who might be involved in them and see if we can find where these emotions fit in," I suggested.

"We know people were upset with him finding their mushroom areas," Mary said. "Fear of them being found, angry when they were revealed, hatred that he was doing it."

Gertie shook her head. "There are many serious fungi hunters in the area. That's a lot of people to have to sort out."

"Peter was very upset," I said. "We should put his name up there."

The Professor wrote it on the chart.

"What do we know about sinker logs?" Rudy asked.

I explained what they were.

Ivan frowned. "What kind feelings go with wet logs?"

"They're worth a lot of money," I replied.

"What comes to my mind is greed, because of their worth, and fear of getting caught stealing," I said. "Rumor has it folks are harvesting them illegally."

Mary picked up one of her cookies. "Do we know anyone connected with them?"

"Roger Simmons buys as much as he can and wishes he could get more, so his name should be on the chart," I said. "Peter needs to go there as well because he's been selling them, and he certainly fits the profile of someone with anger issues."

The Professor moved to the third chart labeled *Native American Sacred Land*. "Daniel's the only one we know who is connected with the sacred site piece."

"He's looking into that," I said. "When we decide on our next meeting, we can invite him to join us and share what he's found out."

The Professor sat at the table. "Ned was probably working on other areas we know nothing about, but this is a start."

A meager one, I thought. Then I realized we needed to start another paper. "Let's make a new chart and label it *other*."

Once again I hated to pull Elise into it, but she certainly bore some ill will where Ned was concerned, as did her son. I filled in the Sentinels with what I knew and the names Joey and Elise were added to the chart.

"Let's put Joey's name on the log list as well. He's been helping Peter," I said.

The group surveyed the lists.

Gertie raised her hand. "I'm meeting with my organic gardening club this afternoon. I'll see what I can find out about the mushroom hunters. Many of the members search for fungi, and they know a lot of people involved in that activity."

The Professor wrote her name on the mushroom chart.

"Ivan and I can talk to the people at McMahon's Wood Shop," Rudy said. "We've been to it several times lately."

"Yah. We go there for *Nadia*. Building special chest," Ivan said.

"Ivan's creating a new storage box," Rudy explained, "and we've had to replace certain areas on the boat. Salt water is hard on it and can cause a lot of damage."

The Professor placed their names on the log list. "I'll make a visit to Mr. Mushroom." He wrote his name in the appropriate place.

I laughed. "Mr. Mushroom? Really?"

The Professor grinned in return. "Yes. He's a retired professor who buys and sells mushrooms and herbs. We get together for coffee and chats."

Mary nibbled on her cookie, a puzzled look on her round face. Then she brightened. "The Friends of the Library have been discussing doing a fund-raising dinner. I'll make an appointment with Elise and see what she would charge to cater it and ask her some questions at the same time."

They each had their assignments. As usual, the well-oiled machine known as the Silver Sentinels had come together with a plan. I was relieved to see action could take place so fast.

"Thank you for jumping in so quickly. I'll let Daniel know what's planned."

I pulled the charts from the wall and rolled them up. "I'm spending the afternoon doing three of the events. I'll keep my eyes and ears open. I'll be looking through a different lens with Daniel being in danger."

"Good idea, my dear," the Professor said. "A different perspective can often lead to new discoveries."

I tucked the charts at the back of the cupboard. "I can't imagine any reason for the people we've mentioned to come into this room, but to be safe, I'll put our ideas out of sight. You know where they are if you meet without me."

"You can never be too careful," the Professor said. "Everyone, please remember our gathering tonight at my place to spend some time with Timothy and Clarence. Mary and Gertie, I'll pick you up as discussed."

Gertie stood and picked up her cane. "Thank you, Professor."

The Professor looked at me. "Scott is coming to the party. I spoke with him today, and he mentioned you'd be having dinner with him tonight. Helen's making a pecan pie for me. I'm happy to pick up the ice cream when I come for the pie this afternoon. That will save you from having to come back here."

"Ohhh…dinner with Scott." Mary breathed the words more than spoke them.

My face heated. *It isn't a date*, I started to say. But actually, it was.

I busied myself straightening the room. "Thanks, Professor. I'll take you up on that."

They took the dishes and beverages to the kitchen and gathered up their belongings, chatting about how eager they were to get to their tasks.

I picked up the bread from Gertie and went to my living quarters. I tucked the bread away and changed for the horseback riding portion of the day.

The idea that the natural inclination for people might be to think Daniel killed Ned to protect Allie was frightening. Even if it was understandable, it was still murder and Daniel would pay a heavy price if found guilty. He might be arrested because of what could be perceived as the strongest motive—along with his threat, written in Ned's handwriting.

I shuddered. Being behind bars and away from Allie and the outdoors would kill him. And once he was put in jail, would he ever get out? Jail brought dangers all its own. I gritted my teeth. I'd be asking questions this afternoon, and a lot of them.

Chapter 11

Helen was bending over the granite-topped kitchen counter focused on what looked like ornate pearl brooches. Had she taken up jewelry making? I went over to see what she was working on. On closer inspection, I realized they weren't pins, they were cookies. And what amazing cookies they were! No wonder the kitchen smelled so heavenly.

The ones I looked at had rows of white frosting in small intricate patterns, their centers filled with what appeared to be pink and white pearls. A miniature rose rested on green leaves off to one side of the palm-sized cookies. A variety of ingredients and unusual tools had been neatly arranged on the counter. Jars labeled *luster dust* had gold, bronze, and pink powder in them. A large container of meringue powder sat next to a marker of edible ink.

"Helen, I've never seen anything like these. How do you do it?"

Helen straightened and put down the pastry bag she'd been holding. "You buy what you need and then you practice, practice, practice."

"I thought they were pieces of jewelry at first."

"I've been hired to prepare cookies for a Victorian tea party in a couple of months, and I thought it would be fun to try something new. I took a few online courses. I'm making these for the church bazaar to sell tomorrow after the contest."

"And I'm making these," Tommy piped up from the work area.

I looked over at the dining table and saw Tommy, with Fred as an interested audience. The basset hound had an ear-to-ear smile on his face and his wagging tail was in overdrive.

I went around the counter and looked at Tommy's project. Here were cookies as well, but these were shaped like dogs. Not surprisingly, most of them looked like Fred, but one had big ears and a tiny body. A pink icing collar around her throat made me figure I was looking at a version of Princess.

Tommy picked up one of several brushes on a plate. "Mom asked if I wanted to decorate dog-shaped cookies, and I said yes. It's fun!"

Helen had come over to observe his work. "These are for people. I found recipes for dog cookies and safe decorating ingredients, and I've been experimenting with those. That'll be the next project. Fred's been giving me feedback."

That explained Fred's happy demeanor.

Bowls of icing were lined up on both sides of the cookies Tommy was decorating. Starting with white, the containers had progressively darker shades of brown, with black at the end. One dish filled with pink frosting had been placed over to the side.

"Mom and I are going into business together." He started putting eyes on a Fred cookie. "I'm going to donate all my money to the local animal shelter."

Helen bent over and hugged him. "One of the women I made a cake for wanted to have some lessons. In return, she's creating a website for me. The baking is a perfect fit for the time off I have in the afternoon."

Tommy piped up. "I'm going to have a mixed breed bag. Mom says it'll be a baker's dozen. And people can also choose to have special ones made up in the shape of their dogs."

I picked up one of the metal cutters on the table, being careful to not let the Chihuahua's sharp ear prick my finger. "Who makes these cookie cutters? They're so clever."

Tommy put his finished cookie on a tray. "Daniel. He said he'd make any breed I wanted."

Daniel. My lighthearted moment came to a screeching end. Time to leave.

"Your cookies look fantastic." I tried to keep my voice upbeat. "I'm off to my next event. See you later."

Tommy's business would come to an end before it began if Daniel landed in jail.

I parked the truck at the contest meeting place and walked to where a row of horses had been tied to a long trailer. One of them had a white rump with different-sized black spots covering it. I hoped it was the leopard Appaloosa I had ridden once before.

I approached a tall, rangy young man. "I'm Kelly Jackson, and I'm registered for this event."

"Hi, there. Diane saw your name on the list and had us bring Nezi for you."

"Great!"

Diane, the owner of the stable, and I planned on getting together for a ride as well as planning a horseback-riding event that included Redwood Cove Bed-and-Breakfast. I hoped we'd be able to do that soon. I gave a sigh of pleasure at my new career. The joy dissipated when I saw Daniel in the distance. I focused my thoughts on how I could help him. For a start, I'd question the cowboys when we got to our destination and see if they knew anything.

The riders assembled, and I joined Timothy and Clarence while they waited for their mounts.

One of the men approached, leading a rawboned bay mare. "Clarence, I saw on your form you're a beginner."

"That's right." He gave a nervous laugh.

"Martha here is real gentle. She'll get you off to a good start."

He helped Clarence mount the long-legged horse. Another wrangler brought Timothy his ride for the day, a palomino quarter horse.

I stepped forward. "I'll adjust their stirrups if you want to go ahead and help the others."

"Thanks. Appreciate that," said the man who had assisted Clarence, and he headed to the next rider.

I shortened Clarence's stirrups and lengthened Timothy's. As I wasn't an employee, the cowboys came by to double-check my work and be sure the mandatory safety requirements were met. I mounted Nezi, and the group began a slow walk to the outskirts of town.

"Have you ever ridden before, Clarence?"

"No." He looked at the ground. "That looks a long ways away."

"We'll just need to be sure you don't meet it unexpectedly," I said.

He flashed me a brief smile, which quickly disappeared as he gripped the saddle horn with white knuckles. His fingerprints might be permanently imprinted into the leather. The horse pulled at the bit and the reins came out of Clarence's hands. I reached over and grabbed them, glad someone had tied them together.

I handed them to Clarence. "Here's how to hold the reins."

I demonstrated for him.

"But then I can only hold on to the saddle with one hand."

"Right."

"But...but..."

"I'll stay with you, Clarence."

Timothy appeared comfortable on his mount and had gone on ahead, chatting with one of the other riders.

Clarence gulped. "Okay."

On we went, Clarence gripping the saddle and occasionally swallowing hard. We wound our way up a dirt path behind the town, leading into the hills. Clarence slumped in the saddle like he was in a rocking chair, a look of discomfort on his face.

I showed him how to put his weight in the stirrups, both to help the horse go uphill and to make him have a more secure seat in the saddle. Unfortunately, that was more than he could handle. Holding the reins with one hand was as far as he was going to go in terms of learning to ride today.

"We're almost there," one of the cowboys called out.

The horses broke into a trot, no doubt knowing a stopping point was ahead and maybe a chance for a snack.

The tall mare's jarring trot turned Clarence's pained expression into one of agony as his bottom pounded the saddle. He let go of the reins and held on to the saddle horn with both hands. He began to slip.

Clarence gave a terrified yell. "I'm going to fall!"

I grabbed the reins and pulled the horse's head to my knee, forcing her into a walk as I slowed Nezi. I reached over and helped Clarence right himself in the saddle.

"Thank you, Kelly." His words were choked and shaky.

Ahead of us, the group had stopped and the wranglers helped people get off one at a time and tied the horses to a rail. One of them approached us. I figured Clarence might have a problem getting off the horse. I dismounted and tied Nezi up.

Clarence took his right foot out of the stirrup.

"Hold on," I said to him. "We'll help you."

Between the two of us, we guided Clarence's descent and held on to him as he wobbled a bit upon reaching the ground.

He steadied and straightened. "Thanks."

He walked away, teetering from side to side on temporarily bowed legs. At least his would straighten out. They weren't like the permanently bowed legs I was used to seeing on the seasoned riders I knew in Wyoming.

The lead cowboy gave everyone maps and directions, as had happened with the mushroom hikers in the morning. "We'll meet here in half an hour."

Timothy and Clarence walked off together. I joined Diane's men, hoping I could learn something. They had settled in a grassy clearing with several wooden picnic tables.

A leathery-skinned man in a denim jacket pulled playing cards from a pocket.

I went over to him. "Nice area."

"Yeah." He began to shuffle the cards as the others settled on the bench seats. "We do rides here regularly and have a picnic lunch at this stop. The property owner charges Diane a small fee for using the area." He dealt the cards.

"Are any of you into mushroom hunting?" I asked the group.

Negative shakes of their heads all around. They stared intently at their cards, some arranging them in their hands in a different order.

I decided to ask one more question before leaving them to their card game.

"I've heard someone talking about sinker logs. Do you know anything about those?"

"Nope," said the card shuffler. "Who wants to start?"

Clearly time for me to leave. "Thanks." I wandered back to Nezi.

That was a bust. Maybe I'd do better with the canoers. I petted the horse on his neck, then let him rub his head on my shoulder, while waiting for the group to return. I didn't mind a few white horse hairs on my fleece. The riders came back on time, and we went through the mounting process.

Clarence didn't want to get back on. He finally agreed when I assured him I'd lead his horse and we wouldn't have a repeat of the earlier incident. He could even hold on to the saddle horn with both hands all the way back. Clarence winced as he settled in the saddle. We had an uneventful trip back.

"That's one form of transportation I will *not* be using tomorrow," Clarence said once he was back on firm ground. "The canoeing starts in thirty minutes. I'm off for coffee."

"I'll join you," Timothy said. "Kelly, what about you?"

"I'll pass. I'll meet you at the starting area for the canoes. I have something I want to do."

Timothy nodded. "Okay. Clarence and I are going over together. We'll see you there."

I stopped by the market and bought a half gallon of deluxe vanilla bean ice cream, dropped it off at the inn, and then followed the directions I'd been given to the launching area. A wooden sign with PADDLER'S PARADISE on it confirmed I'd reached my destination. A row of canoes lined the beach with a pile of life vests in front of them.

Five people stood in a group. Three men wearing black shirts with the canoe company's logo picked up life jackets. I joined them as one of the guides fitted Clarence into his vest. Max sat in front of him, watching the proceedings with a tilted head and wagging tail.

"Max looks happy," I said.

"Yeah. I started canoeing at home with him. Originally I did it in preparation for this contest, but now it's become something we regularly do. Even after I learned enough of the basics for this trip, we kept going out. We stop at different places, and he gets to run around and check out the new smells. I get to absorb the beauty of places I can't drive or hike to."

I checked my cell phone for messages but saw there was no reception here. I'd been told phones wouldn't work more than about two miles out of town. More learning about Redwood Cove. We had issues with service on the ranch at home, so it wasn't the shock to me it might have been for some people who completely relied on it.

The guides paired me with a young man in wire-rimmed glasses. He introduced himself and explained he was learning to be a mycologist. He offered to take the front and help with the steering, explaining he often went canoeing with his parents. I said fine and was happy with his offer. I had paddled some but wasn't an expert, by any means.

The guides gave directions and demonstrations on how to use the oars. A Paddler's Paradise crew member would be rowing at the back of each canoe.

I got into the middle of the boat. One of the guides pushed it a few feet into the water. My partner got in the front, and we were shoved the rest of the way into the water, with the guide getting in the back. We began to paddle.

I was pleased to discover my partner wasn't a talker. The slow glide through the water was soothing. My nerves needed that, as did my questioning mind. I allowed myself to sink into the healing experience. The rhythmic movement of the paddling was like a physical mantra, with the lapping of the water against the canoe providing nature's background music. The gentle flow of the river rocked the canoe back and forth ever so slightly, reminding me of a baby's crib.

The leaders had chosen an easy section to maneuver, probably because they had a range of abilities amongst the group. Timothy and Clarence's canoe moved slowly past us. They smiled and waved. Max sat like he was at attention, the gentle breeze ruffling his curls. A golden-haired king sailing by with his servants rowing him to his destination.

I peered into the water and saw a submerged log. Glancing up to my left I saw a knoll. I was almost positive that was where Daniel and I had stood and this sunken wood was what I'd seen from above. We landed on a sandy beach. I got out and helped pull the canoe out of the water.

As people took off their life vests, I went back to the shore. Bushes down to the water's edge lined the river. Wildflowers dotted the grassy areas adjacent to the sand. Their delicate scent sweetened the air. A couple of butterflies danced in the afternoon sun. I walked over to where the brush began and saw what had once been a road but was now two narrow dirt paths disappearing into the growth.

The routine from earlier trips was repeated as the leaders handed out maps and gave instructions. Members of the party ambled down the twin tracks.

My plan was to stay and ask questions. I could come back and explore the area another time on my own. The three men leading the group sat on a large beached log, and I joined them.

"I'm Kelly Jackson, new manager for Redwood Cove Bed-and-Breakfast. I'm participating in the events to learn more about the area, not to hunt mushrooms."

The men gave me their first names, and I met Mike, George, and Ralph. They commented they were familiar with the inn.

I settled on the log. "This is a beautiful place. Is it part of your regular tours?"

Mike nodded. "It's one of them. We have a variety of trips for people to choose from, depending on their ability and what they want to see."

We continued on for a few minutes discussing their tours, when they operated, and rates. I asked for brochures, and Ralph said one of them would drop a stack off at the bed-and-breakfast.

We sat quietly, soaking up the sun.

I pointed to the knoll. "Is that where the sacred Indian site is located?"

"Yep," George said.

I didn't question people for a living, and I felt uncomfortable about prying into people's lives. But I had to. Daniel needed my help. How did you begin asking questions about murder in the middle of a casual discussion?

"I was there yesterday afternoon." I paused, then plunged ahead. "Did you know a man was killed there last night?"

Their heads snapped around in my direction, and they sat up straighter. Mike leaned forward. "What happened?"

"They don't know yet. Someone shot a newspaper reporter named Ned Blaine."

"I heard he was shot but didn't know where it happened," Ralph said.

We all stared at the top of the hill in front of us.

"Did any of you know him?" I asked.

Mike frowned. "I wouldn't say I exactly knew him. We had a canoe go over. Some teenagers playing around. Wouldn't stop when we asked them to. No one was hurt. He questioned me about it and wrote a story. To my way of thinking, he added a little too much reporter drama."

"Didn't seem to hurt business," George commented. "We changed the wording on some of our forms. That was all that happened as a result of it."

I looked at the knoll where I'd stood yesterday. Their gazes followed mine.

"Eerie to think he was killed up there." I pushed forward again, despite my discomfort and feeling awkward. "Were any of you here yesterday? Maybe one of you saw something?"

George shook his head. "We had a meeting in the morning, then spent the rest of the day preparing for today and tomorrow."

Conversations growing in volume announced the return of the mushroom hunters. Timothy, Clarence, and a prancing Max appeared from one of the small paths in the undergrowth.

We proceeded to repeat that procedure we'd used when embarking on the outing. I wasn't getting anywhere fast. The only thing I'd learned was that maybe Ned overdid things a bit at times. I hoped the Silver Sentinels were having more success. Soon we were back at our launch site and shedding our life vests. Clarence pulled a small soda bottle from his jacket pocket.

Suddenly Max began barking nonstop and lunging at his owner. Clarence turned pale, slowly sank to his knees, and then toppled over into the sand.

Max began pawing at his owner's foot. The dog moaned and then began pawing with both feet as if trying to dig a hole through Clarence's boot.

What is happening?

Chapter 12

I knelt down beside Clarence. His eyes had a faraway look. Max kept pawing at his foot.

A soda bottle.

A frantic dog.

A fallen man.

I think I knew what was happening.

"He might be having a diabetic low," I shouted. "Sit him up."

The canoe guides leaped into action and had him upright by the time I'd taken the top off of the soda.

"Clarence, take a sip." I held the bottle to his lips.

He opened them slightly and I poured a small amount of soda into his mouth. He swallowed.

"Another one."

Clarence obediently complied. He still had a vacant-eyed look about him. I waited a few seconds and we repeated the process.

He blinked and stared at me. "What happened?"

"You tell us." I explained what had taken place.

Timothy had raced over when Clarence had fallen, and knelt beside us.

Clarence blushed. "I'm diabetic. I let my blood sugar get too low."

Max lay down with a moan and put his head on Clarence's leg.

Timothy grabbed his friend's hand. "Clarence, you never told me."

"I know. I'm embarrassed. I brought it on myself. Family members have had problems. I know what I should do in terms of weight and exercise, and I haven't done it. My will power's too weak."

"Ridiculous. I remember when we started the knitting classes and were sharing photographs and stories of our challenges. You were bound and determined to conquer the battle of the knitting needles, as you called it. You can conquer anything you put your mind to."

"Timothy, you're so kind. I'm lucky to have a friend like you. Maybe you can come and stay with me for a while in Oregon and give me that pep talk every day when I reach for a doughnut or a bagel and cream cheese."

"I just might take you up on that. We're going to work out a plan for you to take charge of this part of your life."

Clarence smiled at him. The color had returned to his face. Max was quiet and still next to him.

Clarence looked at me. "How did you know what to do?"

"One summer on my parents' ranch, we had a diabetic guest. He asked to bring his service dog. We don't allow people to bring their pets, but this was different. We said yes. He explained to us how his diabetic alert dog worked. Since he couldn't take the dog on horseback rides, he taught us what a diabetic low looked like and what we should do."

Clarence nodded. "Lucky for me." He began to stand and Timothy and I helped him. "Thanks. Once my sugar is back up, I'm fine." He patted Max's head. "He began pawing, which is his signal to me, but I put off doing anything. I thought I could make it until we beached the canoes."

"Clarence," Timothy said, "maybe we should call it a day."

"No way." Clarence took a long swig of the soda. "I'm not going to miss out on off-roading."

Timothy frowned.

"Honest. I'm all right now. I'll even test myself to be sure."

Timothy raised his eyebrows and smiled. "Okay. I just don't want these competitions to end. I would never have learned how to knit a scarf and beanie without you as my contest partner."

They shared a laugh.

The group had gathered around us when Clarence first fell, then wandered back to what they'd been doing when Clarence began explaining his condition. The guides had gone back to work on the canoes.

"Does Max have a service dog vest?" Timothy asked.

Clarence sighed and ran his fingers through the dog's curly hair. "Yes, but I rarely put it on him. I only use it when I want him to be able to come with me in places where dogs aren't allowed."

"Why don't you keep it on him?"

Clarence let out a longer, louder sigh. "For the same reason I never told you. I don't want people to know."

Timothy put his hand on his friend's forearm. "Maybe this is where you take your first step to change. Acknowledging your condition. Besides, you'll be giving people a chance to learn about diabetic alert dogs. Maybe that will help someone who is struggling with the disease."

Clarence shook his head. "I don't know if I'm ready to do that."

"How about this," Timothy said. "You put it on him for the next event. That way he'll be able to go with you, no questions asked. You can take it off when it's over."

Silence ensued.

Finally Clarence said, "I'll do it. I know I need to change. I could die, and that would leave Max homeless. I can't take that chance. We take care of each other."

The three of us walked to our vehicles. Clarence unlocked his truck, reached under the driver's seat, and pulled out a blue vest with SERVICE DOG printed on both sides.

"Come here, Max." Clarence held it out.

The dog rushed to him, wiggling from one end to the other. I couldn't quite tell with all the long hair on his face, but I thought he was smiling.

"It seems like he's excited about wearing the vest," I said.

"I agree," Clarence replied. "I think it makes him feel special. He struts and prances when he has it on."

Clarence then took out a plastic container with MAX written on the top and gave the dog a biscuit.

Timothy took out the directions to the last event we'd signed up for today, which started in half an hour. The guys were going to stop for coffee. I decided to go on ahead and see what I could find out before the off-roading started. Clarence, Timothy, and Max got into Clarence's green Toyota pickup. Max sat in the middle with the same upright posture I'd seen in the boat.

I arrived at the site of the next event—a parking lot adjacent to a beach. The tide was going out and strings of glistening seaweed littered the packed sand. The salty smell of the ocean drenched me with its pungent scent. A black-and-white bird hopped on orange legs in search of bugs.

I recognized Elise's son's vehicle, with its oversize tires and winch on the front. Three other trucks were parked in the area. A group of men had gathered next to the vehicles. Joey appeared at the side of his truck and put a sign against the back tire that said HAPPY TRAILS OFF-ROADING COMPANY.

"Hi there," I said.

He looked up and smiled. "Hello, Ms. Jackson. It's good to see you again."

"Please, call me Kelly. I didn't realize you were going to be part of this event."

"Yeah. My friends and I started a tour business. It's a chance for us to advertise."

"I've been collecting information about different activities I can share with my guests. Please tell me about what you have to offer."

"We do a variety of trips. It depends on what people want to experience. For example—"

"Hey, Joey, we're meeting now," one of the men called out.

"I have to go. We need to work out some details of the drive. I'll tell you more later." He left to join the others.

Clarence pulled in and parked next to me. The three of them got out. Max trotted around…and around…and around. It was like he was saying, *Everyone look at me. I'm wearing this cool vest.*

Others arrived and we were soon getting our instructions. Joey explained this was a "gentle" drive. He went on to talk a bit about what their company offered. People piled into the vehicles. I chose to go with Joey. A balding man wearing a tan sweatshirt with a large brown mushroom on it joined us, filling the truck's cab.

We drove about twenty minutes, often over roadless terrain. I'd ridden on horses a lot in areas without roads or paths, but rarely in a vehicle. I also occasionally helped drive trucks with fencing supplies across pastures, but this was different.

I wouldn't have used the word *gentle* to describe the ride, as I bounced like I was on a trampoline. Joey drove us through ditches and rocky creek beds, water spraying up on both sides. Once again we went uphill, but our beasts of burden were mechanical this time. I'm sure Clarence was much happier.

We parked in a grassy field. Joey gave directions and handed out maps. The fungi foragers marched off.

I walked over to Joey. "You were beginning to tell me about your new business."

"Right."

He explained how they drove people to remote areas that couldn't be accessed by normal vehicles. Depending on what kind of experience people wanted, it could be an easy ride or a rugged one, reminiscent of the Rubicon Trail, where they went over boulders and through streams.

"It's been a great way to get paid for something we love to do."

"Do you have brochures?"

"Yeah. They're pretty minimal right now, since we've just started. We'll do something nicer when we get more money. I'll get you some."

He walked to his vehicle and rummaged behind the driver's seat, then closed the door and headed back toward me. What I needed in addition to his pamphlets was information about our suspects that he knew—Roger and Peter.

He handed me some pamphlets. "Here you go."

"Thanks."

Joey started to turn away. I knew he'd been to Roger's gallery, but he didn't know I had that information.

"Your mom told me you were into woodworking. Have you seen Roger Simmons's collection?"

He turned around. "Yeah, man, cool stuff. I helped Peter deliver some wood, and he showed us his studio and the work area. Man, the tools he has are incredible. I don't have the equipment yet to do anything as polished as he creates."

I continued to pretend ignorance. "I've been learning about sinker logs. Is that what Peter sells?"

"Sometimes. He has a stack of wood in a barn on his property. He sells other types as well."

I pressed on. "I was surprised when I found out how much the logs are worth."

"Yeah." He shifted from one foot to the other and glanced over toward his friends. "They have a lot of unusual colors."

"I understand it's illegal to harvest them without a permit, but some people are doing it anyway. I was told retrieving them can be very dangerous."

His face got a closed expression, and his eyes hardened. "So I hear. Is there something in particular you want to know?"

"No, just making conversation." That sounded a bit lame, even to me.

One of the young men from the group of drivers had taken out a football while we'd been talking. Joey glanced over to where a game of pass and catch had started. I couldn't think of anything else to ask him.

"I'll be sure to put your brochures out."

"Thanks."

He joined the group in time to catch a hard pass to his chest. A short, sandy-haired man bumped him hard. Joey shoved back, and they laughed.

The man clapped Joey on the back. "Sorry you couldn't stay with us to see the game last night. There were some great moves."

"Yeah. I had a chance to earn a few bucks and didn't want to pass that up."

They sauntered over to Joey's truck and leaned back on its red metal side, soaking up the sun.

A new piece of information. Joey hadn't watched the game. Where was he? Did he have an alibi? He was on our list of suspects because of his mom and his connection with Peter.

Another question to answer.

The group returned, and we began the drive back. On our way to the meadow, we had gone up a challenging hill where I'd seen more sky than ground. Downhill I could see where we were going, but at such a steep angle, I wondered if the back of the pickup would come up and flip us over. I decided I was sticking with horses.

I met Clarence and Timothy in the parking lot. "I'm heading back to the inn."

Timothy nodded. "We'll be along shortly for our dinner event."

"Can't wait to try the candy cap mushroom ice cream," Clarence said.

He bent down and began to unbuckle Max's vest. Clarence paused for a moment. "I'll leave it on a little longer. He seems to be enjoying it so much."

Maybe Clarence was beginning to accept what he needed to do to help himself.

We went our separate ways. When I arrived back at the inn, I found Elise in the kitchen preparing food.

"Is there anything I can do to help?" I asked.

Elise wiped her hands on a dish towel. "Sure. How about putting the name cards on the table?"

"Happy to."

Elise reached in her traveling bag and pulled out a stack of placards. Suddenly, she froze and her lips became a tight, straight line. "We won't be needing this one."

She put the cards on the counter, except for one she held in her hand. Elise went to the sink and pulled the recycling bin out from underneath it. She began to tear the name card into little pieces. Her face contorted, and she ripped faster and harder.

I could see the name *Ned Blaine* disappear in shreds as her fury devoured it, letter by letter.

Startled, I said, "Elise, that man was killed. I know you're upset about the restaurant, but—"

"It's not that. He was a blackmailing son-of-a-gun. The world is a much better place without him."

Chapter 13

"Blackmailing! Was he blackmailing you?"

Elise took a pot from the stove and slammed it down on a hot pad. "Forget I said that...please. It just slipped out."

"But it might be important to the police. Maybe the person—"

"I said forget it. The person he was blackmailing had nothing to do with his murder. I know that for a fact."

"But—"

Two class members entered the workroom. "Welcome." Elise acted as if nothing was wrong and hurried over to them.

There'd be no more talk of blackmail for now, but I wasn't going to let it drop.

Helen entered, went to the refrigerator, and pulled out a tray of different cheeses. "Hi, Kelly. How was your day?"

I shoved thoughts of blackmail to the back of my mind. "It was a lot of fun. I've never done so many different activities in such a short period of time. I hiked, went horseback riding, paddled a canoe, and went off-roading."

Helen laughed. "That sounds like a full day."

"Definitely. I picked up a lot of information we can share with the guests. Next week, when we have more time, I'll go over it with you, and we can add it to our binders in the parlor."

"Okay. I look forward to hearing about them." Helen took the plastic wrap off of the platter. "I'll put the cheese and wine out for the inn guests. Incidentally, Phil and Andy arrived. They're in the common room of the Maritime Suite."

"Great! I'll go say hi."

Cheesemonger Andy Brown and wine expert Philopoimen, "Phil," supplied the cheese and wine for the Resorts International inns in the area as well as a number of other local establishments. In addition, they were often asked to do pairings for public and private events. We asked them to cater for our guests when they requested a party.

I shot a glance at Elise. Her back was to me and she was talking to the young couple with animated hand gestures. She was completely focused on them. I got the message there was no room for her to talk with me.

I walked across the parking lot to a two-story building. The bottom housed a working area for our employees, as well as storage space. The upper floor had recently been renovated into four guest rooms and a common area with a table, chairs, and a small kitchen. I'd chosen a seagoing theme for the unit.

When the idea of creating special rooms had been approved, I shared my thoughts with the Silver Sentinels. They had enthusiastically jumped in, listing places where I could find interesting pieces to decorate the rooms. When an accommodation was completed, I took them on a tour.

An ongoing treasure hunt had evolved. The Silver Sentinels scoured antique stores and rummage sales and texted me with pictures when they found something I might be interested in—everything from a collection of leather-bound books to an antique porcelain doll.

For the Maritime Suite, Ivan and Rudy, retired fishermen, tied four intricate sailors' knots for me. I learned Helen was a calligrapher when she offered to write the names of each one. Mary had searched the Internet to find frames for the placards. The end result was a stunning, unusual display on one wall of the common room.

I climbed the stairs and entered the shared room as Andy unwrapped a soft, blue-veined cheese and placed it on a crystal platter, with parsley and purple violets along the rim. He stepped back and eyed his creation, the smile creasing his plump cheeks, delivering a message of satisfaction.

He looked at me. "Kelly, it's so good to see you. Are you ready to do some sampling? I have some new cheeses."

"And I, my dear"—Phil put his arm around my shoulders and gave me a hug—"have a new wine that complements them nicely. One you'll particularly love, because the winery has a dog adoption area setup there."

"Dog adoption at a winery? That sounds like a wonderful idea. Please tell me more," I said.

"First"—Andy cocked one of his bushy gray eyebrows at me—"do you have time for a tasting?"

I glanced at my watch. I could spare a little time before leaving for Scott's place. "Sure. I can stay for a bit."

It had been a while since I'd had a chance to sit with these two learned men and discuss wine and cheese. I always learned a lot from my conversations with them.

Phil picked up a bottle and displayed the label. It had a collage of photographs showing six dogs. They ranged in size from a pint-sized terrier to one big dog that looked like a St. Bernard. Felix, Trixie, Sophia, Tony, Fluffy, and Queenie gazed at me with imploring eyes.

"Dogville Winery started a rescue group a couple of years ago. They thought it would be a great opportunity for people to sample wine and possibly meet the next member of their family—one with four legs."

"I've heard of coffee shops doing that with cats," I said. "This is the first I've heard of a winery providing it for dogs."

"It's a win-win situation. Some come expressly to see the dogs and then end up sampling wine, and with others it's vice versa." He uncorked the bottle and poured a small amount in a glass and handed it to me. "They're doing quite well with both their endeavors."

I sniffed the wine and swirled it like Phil had shown me when we first met. That time he'd taken me on a vertical flight of wines—a selection of wine made by the same winery over a number of years.

I took a sip and found this current event offering smooth, with flavors I didn't recognize. I didn't pretend to be a wine connoisseur and trusted Phil to choose and describe the wine for our guests.

"What do you think?" he asked.

"It's nice."

"Nice?" Phil pointed his finger at me. "Kelly, you are now the manager of a bed-and-breakfast in the heart of wine country. Come, my dear, let's start seeing what else you can discern."

Andy placed a small plate with a couple of cheeses in front of me and a basket of crackers. "Let her nibble on some Grana Podano and Mimolette while you share wine talk."

"Thanks, Andy." I turned back to Phil. "You know it's a foreign language to me."

"And when learning a new language, you need to start somewhere."

I took another sip. "It's crisp, and there seems to be a citrus flavor." I sipped again. "And I think maybe some apple."

He nodded, teacher to a beginning pupil. "Much better! There's also a touch of pear."

"Thanks for the lesson." I put a golden slice of cheese on a water cracker. "Are you doing any events while you're here?"

Andy settled in a chair at the table. "Roger Simmons hired us to provide and serve the cheese and wine for a party tonight and one tomorrow night."

I sat up. Roger Simmons—one of our suspects.

"Have you worked for him before?"

Phil poured some wine for Andy and himself. "A number of times. It's always a joy because he spares no expense. He encourages us to find the best and most unique supplies. We get to sample varieties we rarely have an opportunity to experience."

"How would you describe his interactions with people?"

Andy sipped his wine. "He's always very cordial and treats his staff well. Roger's very organized and contacts us well in advance of any party he's planning. Why do you ask?"

"I met him recently and was curious about him."

And he was on our charts to investigate. Andy and Phil could be an extra pair of eyes and ears, since they would be spending two nights with Roger and his guests. It was quite likely some people would be talking about Ned Blaine's murder.

"I'd like to ask you to assist me and the Silver Sentinels."

I explained what had happened and our concern for Daniel. They were happy to do whatever they could to help.

I finished by saying, "Stolen sinker logs and finding prime mushroom-hunting areas to sell online and in a book were two of the areas the reporter was working on. We know he had interactions with Roger Simmons, Elise Jenkins and her son, Joey, and Peter Smith."

Andy added chunks of bread to the basket. "We met Elise when we arrived this afternoon. I don't know her son, Joey, or Peter. What about you, Phil?"

Phil shook his head. The short, tight gray curls covering his head glinted in the overhead light. "No."

I put my glass down. "I'll be seeing the Silver Sentinels tonight. We'll set up a meeting time for tomorrow, and I'll let you know when it is. Perhaps you'll be able to get together with us."

"We both have deliveries in the morning," Andy said, "but we purposely left the afternoon free in case we had to do additional preparation for the second party. We should be able to attend your meeting for a while if it's noon or later."

"Thank you both so much for helping." I stood. "And thank you for the superb wine and cheese." I turned to Phil. "I enjoyed the lesson and beginning to learn a new language."

We said our good-byes and I trotted down the steps, energized that we had additional assistance. As I neared the back porch, I saw Tommy and Fred on the lawn in front of their cottage. Tommy rolled over and sat up in front of Fred. He did this a second time. Curious, I went over to see what he was up to.

"Hi, Tommy."

"Hello, Miss Kelly."

He turned to Fred. "Roll over," he said, and then Tommy did another roll. Deep furrows creased the forehead of the perplexed hound.

"What are you up to?"

"I'm teaching Fred how to roll over." Tommy repeated his earlier performance.

I suppressed a laugh. Tommy was the one becoming adept at rolling over.

"Are you having any luck?"

"I haven't really started yet. I got instructions from the Internet, and I have a bag of treats. I thought it might help if I showed him what I wanted."

Fred had had enough of sitting still and decided to get in on the game. He jumped up and did a belly flop on Tommy in mid-roll. They began to wrestle, Fred's wagging tail in overdrive. The entertainment from these two never stopped.

I figured the lesson was over for the day. "Good luck." I went back into the inn.

A few minutes later, a knock heralded the arrival of Peter. Maybe I'd have a chance to ask him a few questions.

I opened the door. "Come on in."

"I brought some mushrooms for Elise." He strode in with a basket over his arm.

Elise took the container. "Peter, that was so thoughtful of you."

"I found a whole batch of porcinis. I thought you might enjoy having them. They can be hard to find. They'll make a nice addition for one of your meals at home."

Elise bestowed on him the biggest grin I'd seen from her to date. "Absolutely." The smile disappeared. "But I know they're worth a lot of money, and I can't pay you anything for them."

"No, no. I didn't expect you to. Thank you for inviting me to be part of your class. Your lunch was the best I've ever had."

"Thanks. That's very sweet of you to say that."

Are they sweet on each other?

Elise began removing the fungi. "Thank you for giving Joey some work. We both appreciate it."

"He's a nice kid, and I need the help."

Elise handed him the empty basket.

"I'm looking forward to dinner tonight," he said.

"I hope you enjoy it as much as you did the lunch."

"With you cooking it, I'm sure I will."

A slight blush crept up Elise's face.

"See you in a bit." Peter headed for the door.

I walked out with him. "With Ned gone, your mushrooms can be safe now...unless he already found your areas and posted them on his website."

Peter tossed the basket into the back of his pickup. "I checked his website and blog. My places weren't there, but a lot of others were. I hope that deputy sheriff does something about it."

"But Ned said the property they were on was public land."

He unlocked his vehicle. "Taking the information off the Internet is the right thing to do."

How to segue into sinker logs? Nothing brilliant came to mind.

"I understand. Say, Roger Simmons showed me some of his collection made of sinker wood. I'd like to learn more about it. He said you have some. Can I see it?"

Peter turned to me. "It's not for viewing. Besides, it doesn't look like much until it's polished."

"Do you know anyone else who has some?"

His eyes narrowed. With his light hair and pointed face, the word *weasel* came to mind. If he lifted his lip, would I see sharp, pointed teeth?

Peter's gaze was anything but friendly. "Since you've been learning about them, I'm guessing you found out they're illegal to harvest. All that's left is whatever some people stashed away a long time ago."

"I did hear something about it being against the law to remove them from the water."

"You're asking a lot of the same questions Blaine did, you know—the reporter who got murdered." Peter got in his truck. "It wasn't a good idea for him and it might not be a good idea for you either."

Chapter 14

I gulped.

That sounded and felt like a threat.

Peter slammed the truck's door. He started it, revved the engine, and backed out, his spinning tires pelting me with gravel.

Were his words enough for me to call Deputy Sheriff Stanton? Peter hadn't said he would hurt me. He could claim he was doing me a favor by reminding me about what had happened to Ned. I decided I'd mention the incident to the deputy when I next talked to him. What Peter had said wasn't specific enough for me to call Stanton.

I went back into the inn. More guests had arrived. Elise flitted between people and the kitchen, juggling conversation with cooking. I'd talk with her another time about Ned's blackmailing.

Back in my quarters, I began to get ready to see Scott. I felt anxious one moment and happy the next. My emotions waged a tug-of-war, pulling me one way and then another.

The emotional wounds of my divorce were now scars. They were barriers I needed to jump over if I was ever to have another relationship. Was that something I wanted? I'd been busy spending my time seeking my place in life, my own personal niche. I felt like I had achieved that here at Redwood Cove. Now another life question presented itself.

This wasn't a decision I was prepared to make now. I willed myself to clear those thoughts out of my head and get ready for the evening. Casual was the Redwood Cove dress code, except on very rare occasions. I chose new black jeans, a black scoop-neck top, and a sweater with a pattern reminiscent of a Navajo rug, with its repeated geometrical designs. I freshened my makeup, brushed my hair, and took my down jacket from the closet.

The evening event was in full swing when I entered the work area. Elise had set out numerous appetizers on the dining room table and was finishing the final touches on dinner as people nibbled and chatted. Her son, Joey, was helping to move pans into the sink and taking food from the refrigerator. Peter had returned. He looked at me as I entered, then his gaze slid away and he turned his back to me. I was surprised to see Roger Simmons among the guests, talking with a young man. I walked over to him.

He turned to me. "Hi, Kelly. Did you have a fun day today?"

Let's see. A murder investigation under way. Daniel a suspect. Clarence with a diabetic low.

"You bet. I enjoyed the activities and learned a lot I can share with my guests."

"Good to hear."

I was surprised to see Clarence and Timothy enter, along with Max in his vest. People immediately clustered around them. I could hear them pelting Clarence with questions.

Roger leaned toward me. "Do you know what's up with the dog?"

I explained the incident, not going into Clarence's discomfort about revealing his condition. I was glad to see him being more open about his disease.

"Interesting. I've read about diabetic alert dogs but haven't encountered one."

I looked at my watch. "I need to excuse myself. I'm meeting with a friend."

"I have to leave in a few minutes, too. I just wanted to make a brief appearance, be neighborly and all."

I walked through the kitchen on my way out. Salad plates were being prepared and the dinner dishes lined the counter next to them. I saw two separated from the rest. One had Clarence's name and a sticky note attached saying *diabetic* with the salad dressing in a separate container, and the other one indicated another guest was vegan. Clarence was being true to his promise of changing.

Off to Scott's.

The drive to the community center took about ten minutes. I parked in front of the building, got out, and was greeted by the sweet smell of freshly cut grass. I took a deep breath and looked out at the pasture next to the building. The resident herd of llamas grazed a short distance away.

I walked over and leaned on the fence. A llama head shot up in the air on a slender, long, ramrod-straight neck. The animal gazed at me. I recognized Annie by her brown and white spots. She began trotting toward me.

The Silver Sentinels and I had been given an opportunity to name the llamas, and she was the one I had been assigned. Annie arrived, and I stroked her soft hair, reaching down into the fine, downy undercoat. I'd picked that name because the short, tight, reddish-brown curls reminded me of Orphan Annie. I gave her a last pat and went to the front door. Scott had said to just walk in. It was a community center and open to the public.

I entered the oversize living area with its inviting chairs, couches, and colorful throws. I heard whistling in the kitchen and went in. Scott had his back to me. He was wearing an apron with a neatly tied bow in the back, blue jeans, and a white shirt with the cuffs rolled up.

"Hi," I said.

He turned, and I burst out laughing. A herd of embroidered llamas ran from the top of the apron across his chest and down to the bottom corner.

His blue eyes twinkled. "How do you like the newest addition to my apron collection?"

I smiled. "Cute. Very cute. I think I even see Annie in there."

"You do indeed. Mary made it to thank me for letting you and the Sentinels name them. They come out regularly with treats for their particular llama." He wiped his hands on the dish towel hanging from the band of his apron. "What would you like to drink?"

"Do you have any sparkling water?"

"I do indeed." He went to the refrigerator. "Would you like ice? A slice of orange?"

"No ice, but the orange would be nice."

He poured me a glass, added a piece of orange, and handed it to me. "Thanks for being brave enough to try my new experiment."

"I doubt I need to fear any of your cooking."

"I didn't use any extreme ingredients and there's no raw fish or steak tartar. We've never really talked about what you like to eat. The couple of deli-style meals we've shared didn't lead us to talk about haute cuisine."

Haute cuisine? Seriously? I grew up on a ranch. We ate chow. I could be in trouble here.

Scott stirred the contents of a pan on the stove. "Tonight I made arancini for a starter followed by chicken maltaise." He talked faster than usual, excitement spurring his voice on.

I knew what chicken was, but beyond that, it was a foreign language. First wine and now cooking. Two new languages in one day felt a little overwhelming. My mind drifted, and I felt my eyes glazing.

Scott put the spoon on the counter and turned to me. "I was going to make a verrine—" He stopped talking and stared at me. "Why don't you tell me what you like to cook while I finish putting the meal together?"

"Well…on the ranch, you know, my mom cooked for the family and crew…and other than preparing vegetables, I never really did much in the kitchen."

"Ah," Scott said with a lopsided grin. "So you were a sous chef."

I chuckled. "A fancy title for free family help."

"What about after you moved out?"

"There was college and dorm food."

Scott knew about my divorce, but we'd never really talked about my marriage.

I took a deep breath and dived in. "Then I got married. My ex liked eating out or grabbing food to go on the way home. We had different hours. He taught a lot of evening classes at the university, while I worked during the day. I cooked very little, and I do mean little."

"What's one of your favorite recipes to prepare?"

I cocked my head. "I make a killer turkey burger."

This time Scott had the laugh. "Got it. I'd love to try it sometime." He sprinkled some herbs into the pot. "Would you like to learn more about cooking?"

I thought for a moment. I was creating a new life for myself in Redwood Cove. This was an opportunity to explore something I knew very little about.

"Sure. I think that would be fun."

"I'll start with some simple recipes."

"Simple sounds good."

"I'll choose some that freeze easily so you can put the leftovers away for another meal." He turned the stove off. "The market's deli is above average, but preparing your own food is always better. You can track calories and salt content."

"I'm game."

"Good. We'll find a date to start later." He heaped steaming broccoli into a bowl. "What are you bringing to the party?"

"The Professor didn't want me to bring anything for a number of reasons. We made a compromise, and I'm contributing ice cream tonight and a pie in the future for one of the meetings."

"Maybe that could be your first cooking lesson."

"Good idea, since others will be eating it. I certainly want them to enjoy it."

"Dinner's ready. I set the table in the dining room."

I helped him move the food. A cheerful bouquet of deep pink snapdragons with yellow centers in a large, clear vase decorated the table. Yellow napkins in crystal napkin rings added to the festive spirit.

The arancini appetizer consisted of fried golden rice balls filled with melted mozzarella, mushrooms, and spinach. Scott explained the chicken was a Mediterranean dish with origins in Malta. The chicken literally melted in my mouth, and the fresh vegetables popped with flavor. The quinoa complemented the sauce that added a bit of spiciness.

"Everything is delicious, just as I thought it would be."

Scott smiled. "Glad you like it."

"You mentioned something else you were going to make."

"A verrine. That's a French appetizer with the components layered in a glass container. I chose the arancini instead."

Two llamas observed us through the enormous plate glass window. A white one, the largest of the herd of five females, I knew to be Natasha. Ivan and Rudy named her after a Russian snow queen in tales they'd heard as children. A black one, with a white stripe on her face, the Professor had named Louisa May after Louisa May Alcott, to give a literary touch to the ladies.

A small group of four men and two women with dogs at their sides walked in the field. They went one direction, then turned all at the same time like a drill team. Each time they stopped, the dogs sat. My guess was I was watching a heeling lesson.

I nodded toward the pasture. "How are plans for helping veterans and training PTSD dogs going?"

"Fantastic. There are now six veterans living here and working with the dogs. Two of them have post-traumatic stress disorder, and the dogs will become theirs when they're trained. The others will be given to people in need. They're all rescue dogs. It's a win-win system."

Michael Corrigan knew there was a significant homeless population in the area, many of them veterans. A number of private cottages had been built for the men and women to transition back into society.

"Have any of the vets found jobs?"

"Four of them have part-time jobs and are learning new skills. Two of the men are working on obtaining commercial B drivers' licenses. That way they can drive the vans we'll be getting to shuttle people to and from town, and take the men who don't have vehicles to their jobs."

I was so proud to be part of an organization that supported the community. Michael Corrigan always kept the welfare of others in mind.

Scott continued, "Michael's going to have his meeting of movers and shakers once we're a little further along and encourage them to do something similar."

He looked at his watch, then stood and picked up dishes. "We need to be at the Silver Sentinels' pie party shortly."

"How are you liking it here?" I asked as I helped clear the table. "I know it's very different from what you're used to."

"I'm enjoying it more than I thought I would. It's been fun having time to relax, read, and try new recipes, instead of being on one plane after another."

"I certainly benefited, considering the great meal you made tonight."

"Thanks." He put a pot in the sink. "I've been on the go so much of my life I've never really stopped to think about a lot of things. I'd have to say working with this project is the most meaningful work I've ever done. Seeing these veterans change and the excitement of the townspeople over the classes and services we're going to be offering has been very fulfilling. Michael nailed it when he decided on what to create."

As I put the last plate in the dishwasher, Scott pulled out a pie from the refrigerator—but it deserved a more royal name than *pie*. The chocolate-covered top had thin, clear pieces of candy embedded around the sides. Miniature silver stars had been scattered over the top. I knew they'd be edible after seeing Helen's supplies.

"I need to put a few finishing touches on this." He opened a packet and pulled out an almost-translucent piece of gold paper. "It's edible gold to decorate the pie."

I leaned in to get a better look at his creation.

Scott cut thin strips and placed the delicate pieces on top of the pie. "With the last case solved and no murderers to chase after, what are you and the Silver Sentinels doing with your time?"

The instant, intense heat in my face told me I'd turned scarlet. I knew the investigating we did concerned him.

Scott glanced at me, his eyes widened, and he put his scissors down. "Kelly, what are you and the group of seniors up to now?"

My face flamed even hotter. Could I get any redder?

We'd shared enough meetings at this point he didn't have to ask if I wanted any cream or sugar. He knew I liked it black.

Four pies lined the center of the table, with knives and servers at the ready next to them. China plates with a silver pattern, stacked napkins, and a row of forks rested at the end of the table.

I surveyed the desserts. "These are beautiful. I see the pecan pie Helen baked for the Professor. What are the other flavors?"

Gertie pointed to one with a perfectly browned crust. "Dutch apple."

"Coconut cream was my contribution," Mary said.

I had no trouble recognizing it with the toasted coconut topping.

"Rudy and me work together," Ivan said. "He do crust and I buy jar of rum and brandy mincemeat."

Rudy added, "Ivan needs to give himself more credit. He also grated orange rind to add to it."

"Yah. Not easy. Grated me too." He held up one of his large hands with a scrape across the knuckle.

"Oh, no, Ivan!" Mary exclaimed.

"No worry. I am fisherman. Used to cuts."

The Professor handed me a cup of coffee.

"Thanks," I said. "I don't see us eating all of this pie. What's going to happen with what's left?"

"Mary figured that one out," Gertie said.

"Scott's going to take it back to the center for the veterans and others who work there," Mary said. "They'll have a pleasant pie surprise! That's sure to bring smiles all around."

I sat next to Mary. "Scott will be along shortly. He had to help some people at the last minute."

Mary pulled knitting needles and a project in progress from her bag. On a chair next to her, I spied the pink dog purse with the top open. Princess was curled up in pink blankets. The tan Chihuahua lifted her head, gave me a dreamy smile, and curled up a little tighter. Her collar sparkled with pink rhinestones.

Mary gave me one of her dimpled smiles. "Such a nice young man, Kelly. And to think he's a gourmet cook, in addition to being attractive and a pleasure to be around."

Ever since the Silver Sentinels and I had breakfast at Scott's, they seized every opportunity to point out how nice he was. Five matchmakers at work.

"What are you working on, Mary?" I asked.

"Knitting caps for the veterans. When I finish enough for all of them, I'll make matching scarves."

I ran my fingers over the black skein of super-soft yarn. "That's really thoughtful of you."

"There's a committee that meets regularly to discuss the community center. We decided we'll do a potluck at the end of the month for everyone involved with it. We're going to surprise the veterans at the dinner. Scott's giving us space in the dining room hutch. There'll be a big sign saying 'thank you for serving our country' and a smaller one under it saying 'from us to you.'"

Gertie joined in. "I'm going to give jars of my strawberry preserves."

"Ivan, Rudy, and I are talking to local businesses about what they can donate," the Professor said. "We've gotten gift certificates and a variety of useful items. They're being very generous."

"I think it's great what you and the community are doing." I sipped my coffee, enjoying the taste of the strong, dark roast. "On a different subject, Scott knows what we're working on."

Mary's needles stopped. "How did he take it? I know he wasn't too happy about our last investigation."

"He understands why we do what we do. Scott offered to help, so please keep him in mind when you're planning next steps."

I caught them up on the afternoon's events. Elise's comment about blackmail evoked an *ooh* and Peter's perceived threat brought a drawn-out *ahh*.

"I'm meeting Elise tomorrow." Mary batted her eyelashes quickly a few times and gave a mischievous look. "I can play quite the gossip when necessary."

"What are you thinking of saying?"

Mary looked at an empty chair. "Elise, honey, I know it's awful that reporter died, but…" She lowered her voice. It dripped with sugary sweetness. An image of a Southern belle in a bonnet and ruffled dress entered my mind's eye. "I hear he used the information he gathered to pad his bank account at the expense of a number of people in this town. Maybe he brought it on himself." She gave a self-satisfied nod to the imaginary Elise.

The Professor clapped. "Very well done, my dear. Do you have any acting experience?"

"Many years ago I participated in a few plays with a local theatre company."

I put my coffee on the table. "Did any of you find out anything of interest?"

The Professor nodded. "Mr. Mushroom said the club, the Fungi Finders, called an emergency meeting. Ned Blaine appeared to have targeted their group for finding their mushroom areas. He's going to talk to a couple of the members and see what he can learn."

"Not so good at lumber yard." Ivan's voice filled the room and probably went out the windows for passersby to hear. Quiet and soft-spoken he was not. "Not want to talk. Want to sell."

Rudy nodded. "It was clear no one wanted to talk about fresh sinker logs. More than happy to sell us pieces in storage—for an arm and a leg."

Ivan grinned widely. "I know mean much money."

As a group, we had had fun teaching Ivan idioms which he initially called idiotgrams.

"I didn't get anything from my organic gardening club," Gertie added. "They knew what Ned Blaine was doing, but no one seemed overly upset. I asked a couple of my friends to let me know if they hear anything."

"Are you all available to meet noon tomorrow at the inn?" I asked.

Affirmative nods gave me my answer.

"I'll text Andy and Phil. They might find out something at the party tonight. I'll let Daniel know as well."

"I'll go early and update the charts with what we just talked about. That way we can start on time," Gertie said.

A knock on the door made me guess Scott had arrived.

As he entered the room, I had to agree with Mary. Over six feet tall with dark hair, blue eyes, and a fabulous smile, he fit the attractive category, but what pulled at me was his thoughtfulness and easygoing manner. While what the Sentinels and I were doing bothered him because he was concerned about our welfare, he also respected our decision to do what we felt was right.

That meant a lot to me. It gave me freedom to be me. People who were sure their way was the only way could make life unpleasant.

"Hi, everyone. Sorry I'm late." He placed his creation on the table. The gold strips glittered in the light.

Gertie inspected the pie. "You outdid yourself, young man."

An ornate grandfather clock, with a mirrored back and gleaming brass chimes, stood at the end of the room. The Professor looked at it and frowned. "I'm surprised Clarence and Timothy aren't here yet."

As if on cue, a phone rang on a triangular table tucked in a corner.

"Maybe that's them." The Professor picked up the receiver. "Hello." He listened, the frown growing deeper. "What! Is he going to be okay?"

We all waited, holding our collective breath.

"Of course you can bring Max to my house. I'll see you when you get here." He hung up and turned to us. "Clarence is in intensive care."

"What happened? A diabetic incident?" I asked.

"No. They think he was poisoned."

Chapter 16

A chorus of gasps followed the announcement.

"They think it was from mushrooms," the Professor said. "The doctors believe he'll be okay."

"Do they have any idea how it happened?" I asked. "Elise was very clear about people not eating the mushrooms they picked. She purchased what she cooked from certified suppliers."

The Professor shook his head. "No. Timothy is bringing Max to stay with us. Maybe he can tell us more about what happened."

"Do you know how long it will be before he gets here?" Gertie asked.

"He wasn't sure," the Professor replied.

Gertie stood and addressed the group. "I know this isn't the festive occasion we'd envisioned. However, we can be happy and thankful Clarence is expected to recover. In honor of that, I say let's eat pie."

Mary nodded. "We put a lot of work into these creations, and it's a good time to bring a smile to our faces and send some sweet thoughts to Clarence."

"I agree," the Professor said. "We can't help Clarence right now, but we can celebrate each day we have."

"How did you want us to handle the sampling, Professor?" Mary asked.

"I thought each person could get a plate and fork and take a piece of whichever pies they were interested in."

Rudy distributed the plates, and Ivan followed with the forks. Mary put a napkin next to each person. The Professor retrieved my ice cream and added it to the table with a scoop. We began to take a slice of one pie then another.

"I'm going to try them all," Scott said.

I laughed. "I agree. I don't see one I wouldn't want to taste."

Everyone's plates ended up with five small pieces of pie and a scoop of ice cream. Talking ceased while we savored the delicious desserts.

I examined the slice from Scott's masterpiece. I'd seen the top and its final decorations, and now I could see what was inside. Underneath the glistening dark chocolate lay a thin layer of light tan followed by a thicker cream-colored layer.

I took a bite and savored the different flavors. The delightful taste of a sweet peanut butter mixture paired with dark chocolate was followed by a light vanilla mixture laced with crunchy mini malted balls. I wasn't surprised it tasted as good as it looked. From the appreciative murmurs around me, the others were enjoying themselves as well.

A knock interrupted us.

The Professor opened the door and let Timothy and Max in. His brother had a dog bed tucked under his left arm and held Max's leash and a pail in his right hand.

Ivan and Scott went to help him.

Scott took the bed. "Where would you like this?" he asked the Professor.

"Put it over near the fire. He'll be more comfortable there."

Ivan had taken the pail.

"That's for Max's water. He's already been fed," Timothy said.

"I will fill for you." Ivan disappeared down the hallway next to the dining room.

Timothy looked pale and his eyes were red. Max still wore his vest. Timothy bent down, removed it, and walked the dog over to his bed. He unclipped the leash and Max immediately lay down and curled up, emitting a long sigh.

Ivan returned with the water and put it down near the dog.

The Professor introduced Scott, then pulled out a chair for his brother. "Would you like some coffee? And please help yourself to pie."

"Coffee would be great," Timothy said, then shook his head. "I don't feel like a pie party with Clarence in the hospital. It doesn't seem right."

"Forget the party part," Mary said. "You need to keep up your strength. Don't think of them as dessert. These are nutritious pies." She got up and pointed to the one the Professor contributed. "Pecans provide protein." Mary continued down the line. "Apple for fruit, medicinal dark chocolate, raisins for minerals, and..." She faltered when she came to her coconut cream. "And coconut for fiber."

I applauded her effort but doubted the few toasted curls of coconut constituted enough to be considered nutritional fiber. Gertie took a slice of each and put them on a plate.

She handed it to Timothy. "Mary's right. This will help."

Timothy gave her a weak smile. "Thanks."

"Please tell us what happened," the Professor said.

Timothy had taken a bite of the pecan pie. He chewed it slowly, then swallowed. "Just as we finished dinner, Clarence began to sweat, his face flushed, and his eyes began watering."

Timothy proceeded to recount what had taken place. When Clarence had started to speak, he sounded confused and disoriented and said he felt nauseous. Clarence stood, staggered, and almost fell. One of the class members grabbed him and helped him to the floor.

It turned out the person was a doctor. He instructed his wife to get his medical kit. He asked Clarence some questions, including whether or not he had any allergies. His wife came back and the doctor took a vial out of his bag and injected Clarence. The doctor told the group he believed Clarence had ingested the toxin muscarine, found in various mushrooms, a poison with very distinctive symptoms.

When planning for the class, the doctor had studied poisonous fungi and had come prepared to help if anyone became ill. Muscarine poisoning usually wasn't fatal, but it appeared Clarence had been hit exceptionally hard. Timothy ended the story of what had happened by telling us Elise called 911.

"Does anyone know how he might have gotten poisoned?" I asked.

"No idea," Timothy replied. "Elise asked him if he'd eaten any of the mushrooms he'd picked, and he said no. I assured him I'd look after Max. I got his truck keys from him because that's where all of Max's supplies are kept."

"How long will he be in the hospital?" Mary asked.

"They're not sure." Timothy put his fork down on his now clean plate. "I'll go see him tomorrow morning. The doctors said he might have died, and the treatment he received at the inn probably saved his life."

The group fell silent on that somber note.

Mary spoke first. "We're certainly all glad he's on the road to recovery." She picked up Timothy's plate. "Would you like some more pie?"

"No, thank you. But I do feel better. You were right about needing to eat something. I didn't get through the whole dinner."

"Timothy," the Professor said, "I'm happy to fix you something to eat."

"I'm fine now. Thanks for the offer." Timothy's shoulders sagged. "It's been a long day. I'm ready to take Max for a walk and call it a night."

"I feel the same," the Professor said. "It's been a long day for all of us, too, and we have a busy day tomorrow."

I thought of Daniel, our worries, the questioning we'd been doing. Yes, a long day.

"I'll take Max for a walk," I said. "You take it easy."

"Thanks, Kelly," Timothy said. "I had to leave my car at your inn. Is that a problem?"

"Not at all. Don't give it another thought."

"Okay." Timothy slumped in the chair.

"There's an empty lot across the street," the Professor said to me.

"Got it." I went to retrieve my coat from the closet.

The Professor picked up the ice cream, entered a room bordering the living area, and flipped on a light. I saw the kitchen with a counter separating it from the living room.

The Professor opened the freezer. "I'll take you ladies home as I promised as soon as Max and Timothy are settled."

"I can drive them," Scott volunteered. "I have the company Mercedes, and there's plenty of room for people and pies."

"I greatly appreciate that, Scott," the Professor replied.

Mary put the dog purse on the floor and took Princess out. "Stretch your legs a bit, baby. We'll be leaving soon."

"Let's pack up the pies," Gertie said.

Everyone began moving. Mary and Gertie retrieved boxes they'd used to transport the pies. Ivan cleared the table, and Rudy rinsed the dishes.

Princess acted the true Chihuahua and went over to check out the much bigger Max. Their difference in size seemed to mean nothing to her. Max gave her a lazy wag of greeting. Princess did a tentative nose touch. That completed, she went back and lay down next to her carrier.

Scott helped the women arrange the pies in the boxes and secure them in place with small air bags Gertie had brought so they wouldn't move around.

"Good thinking to bring the packing supplies, Gertie," Scott said.

Gertie closed the lid on a box. "I always save them when I get catalog orders. Reuse whenever possible, I always say."

Scott took the pies out to the car one at a time as Gertie and Mary finished packaging them.

I picked up Max's leash next to his bed and bent down to pet him. His soft curls were warm from the fire. I clipped on his leash and encouraged the sleepy dog to get up. It took several tries, but finally, with a loud groan, he complied. I saw a large flashlight next to the back door. We had one at the inn in a similar location, always ready for a power failure. I picked it up and turned it on as we stepped outside.

Moonlight flooded the vacant land. A thin wisp of fog snaked its way across the beam of my flashlight, twisting and curling, pushed on its way by the salty ocean breeze. Max's golden hair blended with the tall stalks of dry grass. There were no signs of foxtails that could harm him, so I let him roam on the long leash.

As Max went about investigating, I thought about what had happened to Clarence. Had one of the mushroom distributors made a mistake? If not that, then how did it happen? Could it be possible someone did it on purpose? But why Clarence, the man of many laughs? If it was intentional, had someone tried to kill him?

A mature row of pampas grass lined one side of the area. The fog slithered through the bushy tops of the plants and swirled around me. I felt chilled to the bone as if encased in an icy shroud. Was it from the night air or the emotional coldness of a killer reaching out to ensnare me in its venomous depravity?

Chapter 17

When I returned to the inn, the work area was empty and the kitchen light was on. I walked in there and saw a note on the counter. It was from Elise telling Helen and me she'd be by at one thirty tomorrow to pick up the rest of her equipment.

The parlor was quiet and warm, with a few red embers glowing in the fireplace. Helen had cleared away the evening appetizers and wine and kept the fire going, a job I usually did. With the parties I was attending both Friday and Saturday night, Helen was covering my part. I'd agreed to do full duty Sunday and Monday in return. We had a comfortable working relationship—one I really enjoyed.

I locked up for the night and went to my quarters, ready to call it a day. I texted Phil, Andy, and Daniel about tomorrow's meeting and turned out the lights. What would tomorrow bring?

The next morning I checked my phone for messages and received the welcome news Clarence was out of intensive care. Now that he was coherent, Timothy had asked him if he'd eaten any of the mushrooms he'd picked. Clarence came back with the same answer he'd given last night—no. I readied myself for the day and went to the work area.

As I entered, Helen took a bag of mushrooms from the refrigerator. The smell of frying bacon reminded me of our ranch breakfasts. A bowl of eggs, an evenly browned homemade loaf of bread, a plate of chopped herbs, and another one with a mound of spinach rested on the kitchen counter.

"That looks like a Deputy Stanton breakfast," I said as I poured myself a cup of coffee.

"It is." She began cleaning the fungi with a small brush. "It's my way of thanking him for helping Tommy with his science project."

"It's nice he's been doing that. I can tell how excited Tommy is when he's here."

"With the cancer, my husband wasn't able to do many father-son activities with Tommy. Daniel and Bill have been able to bring some of that into his life." Helen checked the bacon. "I understand someone became ill at Elise's dinner last night."

"Yes, Clarence Norton, the friend of Timothy, the Professor's brother. Luckily, it appears he's going to be all right."

"That's good news. I wonder how it happened."

"No one knows yet. We didn't have a pie party as planned, since it was for Timothy and Clarence. We sampled desserts and went home. How was the book fair?"

Helen put butter and jam on the counter. "It was a lot of fun. Jamie from the Ridley House took care of the parlor for an hour for me. The school had an area where people could swap books, as well as lots of used ones for sale."

"Did Tommy and Allie find anything?"

"Tommy cleaned out all the dog books. He wasn't willing to swap any of his. I'm guessing he spent all the money he saved from his allowance."

"An investment in books sounds like a good idea to me."

"I agree." Helen began slicing the mushrooms. "Allie added a few horse books to her collection."

"Is it okay if I cut off a couple of pieces of bread from that wonderful looking loaf?"

"Of course. Help yourself."

"Thanks. I wasn't sure if you had plans for it."

"It's for our breakfast. It's a new honey wheat-germ recipe I'm trying out."

I sliced off a couple of pieces and put them in the toaster. I retrieved the organic chunky peanut butter and a jar of Gertie's homemade blackberry preserves from the refrigerator.

Helen placed the mushrooms in a frying pan with melted butter in it. After stirring them, she reached for a bottle of dry sherry I'd noticed on the counter and added a splash of it.

"I've seen my mom sauté mushrooms, but she never added wine. Why the sherry?"

"The alcohol burns off and gives the mushrooms a unique flavor."

A nugget of cooking information. Maybe I could impress Scott with it. I blinked.

Impress Scott? Where did that thought come from? Am I beginning to let the gate to my emotions open a bit?

"I'm getting everything ready ahead of time because Bill can't stay today. Too busy. I talked him into breakfast."

I didn't really know anything about Deputy Stanton's personal life. My curiosity was piqued.

I poured myself a cup of coffee. "Does Deputy Stanton have any kids?"

"No. He never married. Said he kept putting his job first and it never happened...and he never found the right person." She flipped the sizzling bacon in the frying pan. "I think it's been good for him to have the interaction with Tommy and not think about his job for a bit."

"Makes sense," I said.

My toast popped up, and I began slathering on the toppings. I took a bite of the hearty bread, peanut butter, and preserves. It was a delicious combination, highlighted by a sip of the dark, strong coffee.

Helen placed the bacon on a plate covered with paper towels to drain. "It's had the additional advantage in that the kids at school are teasing Tommy less. They know Bill is working with him."

A police car drove in and the sturdy frame of Deputy Stanton emerged. He saw me through the back-door window, and I waved him in. Cowboy hat in hand, he entered.

"Hello, Ms. Jackson. Helen." He sat at the counter separating the kitchen from the work area. "Something smells really good."

"There's a spinach and mushroom omelet on the way. Seemed appropriate with all the mushroom-themed activities taking place." She cracked an egg and opened it into a small bowl, checked for any eggshell fragments, then slipped it into a larger bowl. "I read your text about not being able to stay long. This will be ready in a few minutes."

"Sorry I can't work with Tommy today."

"He understands." She frowned and looked toward the door. "He should be here. I wonder where he is?"

I glanced out the back window. "Considering the number of times I've seen him rolling on the lawn in front of your cottage with Fred watching, I think he's still trying to teach him to roll over."

Helen shook her head. "Tommy's the one who's gotten good at that trick."

"You have your hands full. Do you want me to call him?"

"Please."

I opened the back door. "Tommy, time for breakfast. Your mom wants you to come in now."

"Okay, Miss Kelly. We'll be there in a minute."

I liked the informality of the area and encouraged people to call me by my first name. I hadn't done that with Deputy Sheriff Stanton as yet. My dealings with him had involved police business and, at the time, I was a temporary replacement. However, I wasn't temporary anymore, so maybe it was time for a change.

I sat next to the deputy with my breakfast. "Deputy Sheriff Stanton, now that I'm the permanent manager here and working my way up the long ladder to being considered a local, how about calling me Kelly?"

He eyed me for a minute. "Becoming a local, huh? You know that takes years."

"Well, I have officially started."

"Fair enough. Please call me Bill."

I grinned at him. "You're sure you don't want me to call you William, like Gertie does?"

"That's a privilege only my fifth-grade teacher, Gertrude Plumber, has the right to use."

We both laughed.

"I understand there was an accidental poisoning here last night," the officer said.

"Yes, Clarence Norton, a friend of the Professor's brother. I received a text this morning that he's been moved out of intensive care."

"Good to hear. You have to be careful with mushrooms. Some of those LBMs can make you really sick."

"I know what LBBs are—little brown birds—from my birding friends. What are LBMs?"

"Same idea. Little brown mushrooms. There are a lot of different varieties, all looking pretty much the same with only minor differences, and some are poisonous." He sipped the coffee Helen had placed in front of him. "Speaking of the Professor, I'm guessing, with Daniel being questioned, you and your senior crime-solving buddies are checking into the murder of Ned Blaine."

"We are."

He cocked an eyebrow at me. "And, of course, you'll tell me if you find out anything important."

"Right." Was this the time to mention Elise's blackmail comment and Peter's veiled threat? "Actually, there are a couple of things to share. I—"

The short-legged dog and the towheaded boy known as the Fred and Tommy duo bounded into the room.

"Hi, Deputy Stanton," Tommy said, with his outdoor voice still working.

"Tommy, quieter please," Helen admonished him.

"Okay, Mom." He sat in front of the bowl of cereal his mom had put out.

She put a plate in front of the deputy. An omelet garnished with mushrooms and fresh herbs rested on it, along with bacon strips on both sides, and two slices of toast cut on the diagonal.

Stanton sighed, this one a sound of pleasure instead of his usual tired exhalations. "Looks wonderful."

A little pink colored Helen's cheeks. "There's more toast if you want it."

Stanton started eating, then turned to Tommy. "Where are you with your project?"

Tommy began his over-the-top detailed description, as he was wont to do.

I finished my last bit of toast. "I'll go pick up the breakfast baskets."

"Thanks, Kelly." Helen sat on the stool I'd vacated, with her own breakfast of toast and scrambled eggs.

It took several trips to collect the woven baskets with the red checked dishtowels covering the top, which had been filled with breakfast foods for the guests. There were only crumbs left of Helen's blueberry muffins and a little juice in the bowls that had been filled with fresh fruit. By the time I was done, Stanton was just finishing his last bite.

Tommy slid off his stool. "I know you can't stay and help me today. I understand. And the project isn't due for another three weeks."

"I'm sure I'll be able to help you before then," Stanton said.

"I made something for you. I'll be right back." Tommy rushed out, with Fred on his heels.

The officer turned to me. "Ms. Jacks...Kelly, you started to say something when Tommy joined us."

"Right. I had an encounter with—"

Once again I got cut off as the officer's phone rang. He pulled it out, glanced at the screen, and answered. "What's up?"

I tuned the conversation out and helped unload baskets while Helen worked on the dishes.

Stanton slid his phone back into his pocket. "There's an interesting turn of events regarding the poisoning."

I perked up.

"One of the deputies just got off the phone with Elise Jenkins. She says what's left of the salad the poisoned man ate is in the refrigerator and the mushrooms in it were not put there by her. She used a different type."

I opened the refrigerator door and saw a salad at the far back. Elise had pretty much hermetically sealed it by putting several layers of plastic wrap over the whole dish.

I retrieved it and placed it in front of Stanton. "Why did she wait until now to call you? Why not last night?"

"She said her son had been helping her at the beginning of the meal. He'd left before the man became ill. She wanted to check with him to be sure he hadn't accidentally added mushrooms to the salad. He was out late last night, and she didn't get a chance to ask him until this morning."

We stared at the now-wilted salad. I could see several innocent-looking pieces of brown mushroom.

"Did anyone else get sick?" Deputy Stanton asked.

"Not to my knowledge," I said. "I saw some of the people who attended the dinner when I collected baskets. They seemed fine."

"Could Clarence have put them in there? Maybe wanting to eat some he'd found?"

"Timothy said he told them no last night. But he wasn't clearheaded at the time. In the text this morning, Timothy said he asked Clarence again and he said he didn't add anything."

If Elise didn't put mushrooms in there, that means someone else did. Did someone intentionally poison Clarence? What other reason can there be? Sabotaging Elise's class? Why?

"How would someone know which salad was Clarence's, if he was the target?" Stanton asked.

"His salad dish was separate from the others, with his name on it. He's diabetic and his dressing was on the side," I replied.

Stanton stood. "Helen, thanks for the wonderful breakfast. It'll help me through what I'm sure is going to be a long day."

I went and got a bag and put the salad in it.

The deputy turned to me. "Ms. Jac...Kelly." He smiled. "That's going to take some getting used to. Unless you have something earth-shattering, like the name of the killer to tell me from your group's investigation, it'll have to wait while I get this to the lab."

"No names yet. We're meeting at noon, and there might be more information by then."

Tommy ran in and did a practice long slide on a section of the wooden floor, coming to an abrupt stop at the counter. Fred plowed into him and then plopped down.

He held up a bag of cookies for Deputy Stanton to see. "I made these for you."

They were Fred cookies. Tommy even had the spots in the right areas.

He bolted to a drawer in the kitchen and pulled out plastic gloves, like I'd seen bakers use. Helen had trained him well. Tommy dug into the bag. They were all Fred, except for one.

"I wanted to show you this cookie." He pulled out the object of his search. "This is Fred's friend, Princess. I didn't want her feelings to be hurt so I made a bunch to look like her. I'm going to give them to her owner."

He held a Chihuahua cookie with pink icing and a sparkling collar.

Helen said, "I made the cookies, but Tommy did all the decorating. That glitter is edible."

Stanton took the Princess cookie and pulled out one of Fred. "Tommy, you're really talented. I'd recognize Fred anywhere."

A loud tail-on-floor thumping let us know Fred had heard his name.

The deputy placed the cookies back in the bag. "Thanks, Tommy. This will definitely help me through the day, too."

Daniel walked in, holding a box. We'd been so busy I hadn't noticed his arrival. But this wasn't the Daniel I was used to seeing. There was no cheerful greeting or wide smile. His face was expressionless.

He inclined his head toward the officer. "Deputy Stanton."

"Good morning, Daniel," Stanton responded.

"Kelly, here's the rest of the order we were waiting on." He placed the box on the floor next to the back door.

"Thanks, Daniel."

"I can't stay. I have a meeting to attend." He gave a general wave to all of us and departed.

The light moment of dog cookies disappeared down the dark road of Daniel being a suspect. I hoped we discovered the identity of the killer soon.

"Gotta go, too. Thanks again, Helen." Stanton ruffled Tommy's hair. "I'm looking forward to the cookies."

Stanton left and Tommy got down on the floor and began petting Fred. He stopped and looked at me. "Miss Kelly, I forgot to tell you. There's something under the windshield wiper of the truck."

"Thanks for telling me." Puzzled, I left to check it out.

As I approached the vehicle, I could see a white envelope on the windshield. I pulled it out. It was soggy...probably from last night's fog. I opened it carefully so as not to rip the wet paper.

Cut out letters had been glued haphazardly. "Stop asking questions or you'll be stopped."

Simple.

To the point.

I didn't play poker, but I knew someone had just upped the ante.

Chapter 18

My phone rang. I saw Daniel's number in the window.

"Hi, Daniel."

"Is Stanton gone?"

"Yes, he left shortly after you did."

"I have something I need to talk to you about. If I come over now, do you have a few minutes?"

"Sure. See you soon."

I tucked the note in my back pocket. I wouldn't mention it to Daniel. He had enough on his mind. However, this note gave me something new for Deputy Stanton. It was put on the truck last night. Maybe we were closer to finding out something more than we thought…even though we didn't know what it was.

I went into the kitchen and found Helen putting away the rest of the supplies Daniel had delivered.

She closed the cupboard she'd been stocking. "There's one more basket to retrieve. I'll take care of that, then I promised Tommy I'd take him into town. Someone told him there's a mushroom-hunting pig in the contest. He's hoping it'll be at the kickoff breakfast this morning."

"He's right. Her name is Priscilla. She's black and white and yesterday wore a large pink ribbon on her collar. She's a kick to watch. I was told she loves attention."

"Sounds fun. Are you going to go to any of the activities today?"

"I wasn't planning to. I might drop by where the groups meet for a while," I said.

"Okay. I'll see you later."

Helen left, and I poured myself another cup of coffee. Daniel pulled in before I had any more time to think about the note and its potential consequences. He let himself in the back door. A camera case hung from his shoulder.

I held up a mug. "Would you like some coffee?"

He sat where Stanton had been. "You bet."

I poured it and handed the mug to him. "What's up?"

"Remember the sinker log I pointed out to you on our tribe's sacred land?"

"Sure. I saw it again yesterday when I was out with the canoe group. What about it?"

"It's gone, and the shore and adjacent land has been ripped up."

"What?" I put my coffee cup down harder than necessary. "How can that be? How did you find out?"

"Two young men from our tribe went out last night to do a sunset ceremony and everything was fine. They returned to do a sunrise ceremony on the knoll. They saw the damage as soon as the sun came up and called me."

"That's where Ned Blaine was killed. Is that why you didn't want to say anything in front of Stanton?"

Daniel stared into his coffee, as if searching for answers in the dark liquid. "I went out to see for myself. The less said connecting me, the reporter, and the site of his murder, the better."

I nodded. "I understand."

"I took detailed pictures." He pulled his camera out of the case, turned it on, made some adjustments, and handed it to me.

I studied the photos he had taken. The damage to the land was horrific. It was as if some giant, raging monster had slashed its way through, intent on destroying as much as possible.

"How awful, Daniel."

"There's no way I can drive down there in my bus. I've walked in before, but it takes a couple of hours. There's an emergency tribal meeting this morning to discuss what happened and what can be done to restore the site. I took these pictures to show the elders." He sighed. "I'd like to see it up close. Maybe there's even something there to indicate who is responsible."

"I have a thought." The day's schedule of events had been posted on the bulletin board. I took it down and found the number of the canoe company. It was nine fifteen. If they had room, I could still make it on time.

I called them and lucked out. They had a space and, if I could get there by ten, they'd be happy to have me.

I joined Daniel at the counter. "Like I said, yesterday I saw the sinker log when I paddled down the river. The damaged area is where we pulled out the canoes. I'll go and take more pictures and see if I can find anything."

"Are you sure that's a good idea?" he asked. "There's a murderer on the loose and that's near the area where it happened. I know you've been asking questions. Someone might not like it."

A prickle of unease ran down my back. *I know someone doesn't like it.*

"The guides stayed in that area yesterday while the mushroom hunters took off. I'll stay in sight of them."

Daniel had a worried frown. "I don't know, Kelly."

"Daniel, if someone wants to hurt me, there will always be opportunities, short of barricading myself in my room. I'm not going to do that. I'm also not going to take unnecessary chances. I won't wander off into the woods by myself."

"You're right. If someone really wants to hurt you, that's not hard to do."

Thanks, Daniel.

"The sooner we can bring an end to what's going on, the better for everyone," I said.

He shifted on the stool. "You can say that again."

"I've got to get moving if I'm going to make it to the canoes in time."

He finished his coffee. "Right. I need to get to the meeting."

He left, and I rushed to my rooms. I put the note in my desk drawer, changed into shoes appropriate for canoeing, and headed for Paddler's Paradise.

People had their life vests on and were beginning to get into the canoes. One of the guides from yesterday saw me and waved. He reached down and picked up a vest and handed it to me when I got to him. I picked up an oar from the stack next to him.

He pointed to the last canoe in the row. "There's space in that one. We'll work out the payment when we get back."

I nodded. "Thanks."

A red-haired man with a full beard, wearing a blue Paddler's Paradise T-shirt, addressed the group. "My name's Tim O'Brien. I'm the lead guide today. Please listen up, everyone. There is bridge maintenance being done upstream. Debris that's collected on the piers is being broken up and is floating down the river. This shouldn't create a problem for anyone. I'm going ahead to check our landing area and clear it if necessary."

He got in a canoe and paddled off with strong, swift strokes.

I settled in the bow of the canoe and a heavyset man, wearing a long-sleeved denim shirt and blue jeans, took the middle position. A young dark-haired guide pushed the canoe into the water and got in the back. I put my hand in the river and delighted in the feeling of the cool silkiness of the water rippling against my fingers.

The trip was smooth and fast. Sticks and some leafy branches floated past that weren't in evidence yesterday. Our guide easily navigated around them. I recognized a few of the people who had been with my group yesterday. The canoes glided around a corner and came to the landing area.

Our guide abruptly slowed. "What the…"

The smooth sandy beach had disappeared. Large gouges and wide ruts led down to the water's edge.

Tim had beached his canoe and waved to us. "Over to the right," he yelled.

There was a short, undisturbed section of beach up against a row of bushes. We couldn't go in as a group. No more than two canoes could unload at a time. The guides paddled in circles to wait their turn as people got out and the canoes were quickly pulled up on the land.

We were the last to land. I disembarked and grabbed the side of the canoe. The heavyset man did the same on the other side. Our guide took hold of the back. This part of the shore was steeper, and it took some muscle from all of us to get it securely on land.

The mushroom hunters had gathered together and were gazing at the destruction.

A slender man I recognized from yesterday's group appeared stunned. "What happened?" he asked the guides, who were surveying the beach.

"I have no idea," my guide said. "What a mess!"

Indeed it was. Bushes were flattened, their branches crushed. Part of the shore had caved in. The narrow tracks the mushroom hunters had used as paths yesterday were now wide strips of torn-up earth, with broken limbs hanging down from the surrounding plants. My stomach felt queasy at the destruction before me.

"Okay, there's nothing we can do about this except report it later. I know you want to get on with your hunting. You have an hour." Tim urged them on and away from the disturbing sight.

I went over to the shore and studied the damaged land. Several different-sized tire tracks had left their imprints in the mud. I reached for my phone to take pictures.

The sound of an approaching engine from the newly widened road stopped me. Several of the hunters who were about to go down the track stepped aside. A red truck, jacked up so high you could see its undercarriage, emerged. A winch and a spotlight were bolted on the front bumper. The oversize tires churned through the mud and sand, flinging it into the bushes.

Joey.

He drove toward me and pulled into the area I'd been about to photograph. He backed the truck up and did a three-point turn, positioning the vehicle for him to be ready to leave. Joey jumped out, wearing a Giants baseball cap, his wispy blond ponytail protruding from the back. The passenger door opened and Peter emerged. They waved to the guides. Being locals and men of the outdoors, it didn't surprise me they knew each other.

"Hey, man," Joey said to one of the guides. "I heard the place was messed up. I'm working this afternoon, but I had the morning off and wanted to see the area for myself. Any idea what happened?"

"None. What about you? Anything on the grapevine?" Tim asked.

Joey shrugged. "A lot of people knew about the sinker log here. Wondered if there could be a connection."

I already knew the answer but went with the group anyway as they walked to the river. We went as close to the bank as we dared. No log rested on the bottom of the river. Drag marks marred the shore. A musty, earthy smell filled the air.

"There's the answer," Peter said. "Someone finally nabbed it."

The red-haired guide nodded. "Heavy equipment did this damage."

The ruts revealed tire track patterns I guessed to be about two feet wide. I took a couple of pictures and put my phone back in its case. The men continued talking, and I wandered over to where I'd been about to take photos before Joey and Peter arrived. I had seen several different tire tracks. Now the only clear prints were those of Joey's truck.

Peter and Joey were both in the wood business. Did they have anything to do with the theft? Splatters of dried mud covered the truck, including the windshield and up onto the roof. Windshield wipers had cleared the view for the driver. Had this happened on their way here or last night? Had Joey intentionally driven his truck over the tracks?

I walked farther out but didn't find any more tracks. The area became grassy, with clumps of bushes and the beginning of a stand of redwood trees. The grass was matted here, as if something heavy had rested on it. I walked slowly, examining the area. I made wider and wider circles but found nothing. My last pass brought me to the river's edge. No damage here.

I glanced over at the guides. The men sat on the same logs as yesterday, situated in a grassy portion of the landing area at the back of what had been a sandy beach. They were in clear sight. The only place I was going to find anything was where there was evidence of activity...and I didn't see any here.

I stared down at the river, only a few feet away. Suddenly something bumped me hard from behind. I grabbed at a branch of a young redwood tree, but it slipped through my fingers. I teetered on the edge of the bank and then plunged facedown into the cold river.

Chapter 19

The shock of the cold water took my breath away. I flung my head back and gulped in air. The current pulled me away from the shore. Fortunately, I was a strong swimmer and instinct kicked in. I treaded water and scanned the bank where I'd been standing and didn't see anything or anyone.

I began to swim back to land, using a breaststroke so I could keep my head above water and my eyes on where I'd been pushed off. As I got close to shore, I pulled my legs under me and felt the ground. I shuffled a couple of steps, almost neck deep in water, then couldn't move my right foot. It had become entangled.

I twisted, pushed, and pulled, but it was held fast. My bouncy weightlessness didn't give me any leverage. Taking a deep breath, I held it and went under water. I grabbed my calf and tried to tug my foot free from whatever held it. No luck. I pushed upward and my head came out of the water. I breathed deeply for a few breaths then went under again. This time I was able to grab my foot and pull. I felt a tangle of roots encasing it. I had to go back up for more air. By now I was panting.

A stick poked my cheek, causing a flash of pain, then was sucked away by the current. I looked upstream and saw some good-sized branches getting close. Beyond them was a much larger one that could do serious damage. Fear shot through me. I needed to get to shore.

"Help!" I yelled.

The closest branch punched my upper arm and floated away. I was surprised at how much it hurt. The current gave it some strength. What I'd thought was a large branch I now could see was a small tree, its ragged end pointed at me. It was big enough to possibly knock me out, and the branches could force my head underwater.

My heart raced. I willed myself not to panic and cried out again. "Help!"

Joey appeared on the bank. "Person in the water!" he shouted. He took off his hat and tossed it on the ground. He lowered himself into the water, using an exposed root for support, and started walking toward me, using his arms in a swim-like motion to help him move forward. I could tell he was feeling his way along with each step.

He stopped a couple of feet in front of me.

"My right foot is caught," I called to him.

The water came up to the middle of his chest. "Got it."

I glanced up the river. The tree and its companions were getting close.

Joey took a deep breath and dropped under the surface. I felt his hands trying to push my foot free. He surfaced with an explosive exhale, took another breath, and went under again. This time I felt tugging around my foot. He was going after what was holding me in place. The rope of roots loosened, and I was able to push my foot out and to freedom.

Joey stood with another loud release of air.

"That did it," I said.

I took a step forward, and he moved to my side and grabbed my arm, helping me navigate the slippery mud. Two more steps. The branches of the tree raked my back as it passed.

The guides and Peter lined the shore. We reached the bank and Joey let go. The men reached out and pulled us onto the land.

I was trembling from cold and fear, adrenaline still racing through my body. My soaked clothes clung to my skin, driving the chill of the river deep into me.

"What happened?" Tim asked as he took Joey's place and steadied me.

We slowly walked to where the canoes were beached. The rest of the group formed a small crowd around us. Someone threw an oversize sweatshirt over my shaking shoulders and pulled the hood over my soaked hair.

"Something bumped against me and the next thing I knew I was in the water."

Tim frowned. "What could have hit you like that?"

"I have no idea. I haven't seen any large animals in the area," I said.

Other than the human kind. I figured it was a *who*, not a *what*. I shot a glance at Peter and Joey. They had their heads together. One of them, I figured, after Peter's threat and Joey's displeasure.

The guides looked puzzled but had the courtesy to not look skeptical.

"Did any of you see anything?" I asked.

Unanimous shakes of the head gave me the answer.

Tim led me to one of the canoes. He supported me as I sank down on a nearby log.

He took a plastic box out of the front of the canoe and opened it. "We have towels, a thermal blanket, and a medicine kit in here."

He pulled the blanket out. I removed the sopping wet sweatshirt and draped the blanket around my shoulders. It didn't help much, considering my sodden clothes, but I appreciated even a little extra warmth.

I took a towel and dried off the best I could. Rolling my pant legs up to my knees, I massaged my wet, clammy skin with the towel, hoping to get the blood flowing and the return of some warmth. I vigorously rubbed my hair, then finger combed it.

"Do you have any injuries?" he asked.

"I don't know." I put the blanket on the ground. "I got hit pretty hard by one of the sticks."

I took off my fleece jacket and pushed up the sleeve of my top. There were no cuts, but a red spot on my upper arm probably would develop into a fist-sized bruise later. I took off my right shoe and sock and discovered numerous scrapes on my ankle from my struggles.

Tim handed me another towel, a bottle of water, and a tube of antibiotic ointment. "Here's water you can clean with and some cream you can put on those cuts."

"Thanks."

He smiled. "Hey, we redheads need to stick together."

The scratches weren't serious. It took me only a few minutes to take care of them.

"Do you want a Band-Aid to put on your ankle?"

"That's a good idea, with all the sand here. I'll keep my pant leg rolled up to keep it dry."

He handed me a large bandage that covered the injuries. The rest of the group circled around us, watching the proceedings. It appeared the ministrations I was receiving provided their show for the day. Joey was with them.

I looked at him. "Thank you, Joey. It's quite possible you saved my life."

"Just happy I heard your yell. I can take you back to Paddler's Paradise in my truck if you'd like."

I hesitated. Was this a smart thing to do? I suspected Peter or Joey had pushed me in. However, Joey had also saved me, and everyone here had heard his offer of a ride. It would be stupid of them to do anything to me now.

"I'd appreciate that. The sooner I get out of these wet clothes, the happier I'll be. Can we go straight back?"

"Sure. No problem. I'm done here. I just wanted to see what had happened with the sinker log."

I handed the towels, the ointment, and the blanket to Tim. "I'll pay for the trip at your office before I leave."

Tim and the others had heard the conversation with Joey. This gave a time frame and an expectation in terms of when I should be back to Paddler's Paradise. Hopefully, this would prevent the two of them from hatching up any new ideas for getting rid of me if they were responsible for what had happened.

Tim gave me the blanket back. "Keep this. You can turn it in at headquarters."

I put it over my shoulders and clutched it close to my body. "Thanks."

Joey stepped forward. "I have a change of clothes I keep in the truck. You're welcome to put those on."

"No, you use them. You said you're working this afternoon, and you'll need them. I'll be okay. Thanks for the offer."

"Are you sure? I've air dried before."

This brought a chuckle from the guides, who probably had experienced the same thing.

I shook my head. "I doubt if you'd be dry by the time of your event in this cool weather. You use them."

"Okay, then. I'll be back in a jiffy and get you to the Paddler's Paradise."

He disappeared in the woods. While he changed, I pulled my phone from my holster. Had it survived? I unclasped the top and pulled open the seal of the plastic pouch. I took the phone out, pushed the button, and the screen sprang to life.

I checked the photos I'd taken, and they were all there. The ads had said the phone case was waterproof. I was pleased that indeed it was.

The guides still stood around talking and glancing in my direction, as if expecting something else to happen. I wasn't planning on providing episode two of the morning's top story. I thanked them for their help, then put on my tennis shoe and squished my way to Joey's truck.

Joey was true to his word and returned in a few minutes, soggy clothes in hand. He tossed them into the back of his truck, opened a tool box, and pulled out a pair of work boots.

"You really do come prepared," I said.

"Things happen when you go off-roading. Sometimes a truck will go over at a water crossing."

We said our good-byes to the guides, and Peter split from the group and joined us.

He held the passenger door open. "Do you want to sit in the middle in front or in the back seat?"

Squeezed between Peter and Joey was not where I wanted to be.

"Back's fine," I said.

Peter opened the back door for me.

The truck was at least two feet higher than the ones on the ranch. Peter didn't offer to help me in, and I didn't need any. I grabbed the inside frame on the right with one hand, a vertical handle attached to the left side with the other, and hauled myself up.

Peter and Joey got in and Joey turned the heater up full blast. The warm air felt wonderful to my frigid body. I leaned forward to where the heat streamed between the two front seats. I stretched my arms out and held out my hands, palms up.

I'd once been bumped by a surprised mountain lion on the ranch and landed on my side in a corral of spooked horses, but I didn't believe an animal had been responsible for my unplanned swim. The guides had no reason to go after me, whereas the two in the front seat might have a reason for wanting me out of the way. Joey was there shortly after I went in the water and close enough to hear my cries for help.

But if Joey pushed me, why did he save me? Was it Peter? I had looked at the group of men right before the bump but didn't get a good look at who all was there. I didn't think the guides would talk to me about the whereabouts of Peter and Joey when it happened. I was an outsider, and they were friends. However, they might tell Deputy Sheriff Stanton.

We bounced down the track that had been widened into a road once again by whatever mysterious equipment had traveled over it. Some of the ruts were deep and the truck slid a bit as Joey navigated through them. The vinyl seat and my wet pants made for a slippery ride. The seat belt helped, but not much.

"Whoever did this helped our business out," Joey said to Peter. "It gives us a whole new place to bring people. This was way too narrow to navigate before."

"Do you have any idea who did it?" I didn't expect any help but figured I'd ask.

"Nope," Joey said.

Peter shook his head. "Not a clue, but they'll make some big bucks with that log."

I wondered if some of that money would find its way into his pocket and possibly Joey's.

The dirt road came to an end, and I was relieved when we were back on a paved highway. I could see why it would've taken Daniel a long time to walk to the river, and his Volkswagen bus definitely couldn't have made it. The ride to the headquarters and my truck took about ten minutes.

Joey stopped in front of the office.

"Thank you for the ride," I said. "And thank you again for pulling me out of the water." I opened the back door, held on to the bar next to it, and slid out.

"Glad I was there."

Yet, as I closed the door, I couldn't help but wonder if his polite response only hid something more devious beneath the surface.

He turned around and sped off.

Chapter 20

A mini log cabin served as the Paddler's Paradise office. I walked in, paid the bill and returned the blanket, replying to all the staff's questions about what had happened with a simple, "I slipped." I walked to my truck, unlocked it, got in, and turned the heater up as high as it would go.

I headed back to the inn as fast as the speed limit would allow. I parked and entered through the seldom-used side door to avoid meeting anyone. A look at myself in the rearview mirror had revealed a scary sight. The wet clothes were one thing, but the tangled strands of hair gave me a Medusa look.

I went to my rooms and removed the bandage, wincing as it pulled at my skin. After a quick shower and treating my scrapes, I readied myself a second time for the day. I glanced at the drawer that held the threatening note and decided to leave it there. I'd tell the others about it, but the less handling before giving it to Stanton the better.

I called Deputy Sheriff Stanton about the threat and the bump that sent me into the river. He said he'd come by in the afternoon to pick up the note and would stop by Paddler's Paradise to question them as soon as he had an opportunity. Ned's time of death had been narrowed to late Thursday night, and he'd be questioning people again as to where they were.

I promised to tell him what the Sentinels and I had learned, then dialed Scott's number.

He answered after two rings. "Redwood Cove Community Center."

"Hi, Scott. I wanted to let you know Clarence is out of intensive care."

"Good to know. By the way, do you know a man by the name of Roger Simmons?"

Did I ever. His name had a place on our suspect chart.

"I do. Why do you ask?"

"He said he's having a party tonight for the people who helped put on events for the festival and asked me if I wanted to come, to make contact with more locals. He knows about the community center. I thought he might have invited you."

"He did, and I plan on attending."

"Great. I have a business dinner at the time the party starts, but I'll stop by when we're finished eating."

"How do you know him?"

"I contacted him about what we were putting together for Redwood Cove residents and veterans. We discussed ways he could support us. He hired two of the veterans to work as valets yesterday and tonight. We had quite the scramble putting suits together for them, but we managed."

"That was nice of him."

"Yes, it was. I look forward to seeing you there tonight," Scott said.

"Same here."

That certainly came out of my mouth fast.

The conference room was still dark as I walked by to put my clothes in the washer. The light was on when I headed back. A peek inside showed Gertie putting up a piece of chart paper...or trying to. Her diminutive size made it a challenge.

"Let me help you." I took the paper from her.

"Hi, Kelly. This one didn't need any updating, so I wanted to get it out of the way. I have information to add to the others."

I helped her spread them out on the tables. "Timothy texted that Clarence is out of intensive care."

"Wonderful news." Gertie pulled marking pens from a drawer.

"However, it means we need to start a new chart."

I explained to her about Elise's news regarding the possibly poisonous salad.

Gertie ripped a clean sheet of paper off the chart pad and wrote *Clarence* at the top and added *poisoned* with a question mark. "Who on earth would want to hurt him?"

"I asked myself the same question. Deputy Stanton took the salad to the lab. I told him I'd update him after our meeting and maybe he'll know more by then."

Gertie added information to the remaining charts, and I posted them on the wall.

Helen entered with a tray of cheese, crackers, and an assortment of fruit. "I thought your group might need some fuel to feed their thoughts. I'll bring in tea, coffee, and water."

"Thanks, Helen. The treats will be appreciated." I suddenly felt famished. Maybe the unexpected swim, followed by my racing heart, had something to do with it. I took a plate from the stack we kept on the sideboard, cut a piece of blue-veined cheese, and placed crackers and a cluster of red grapes next to them. I took a bite of cheese and savored its creamy flavor.

The Professor joined us with the usual twinkle in his blue eyes, carrying a plastic container. He'd chosen to wear a blue plaid bow tie that matched his wool cap. Mary wasn't far behind with a pink Princess purse in one hand and her personal purse in the other.

She put the portable dog carrier on a chair and lifted Princess out. "Do you like your new coat, honey?"

Princess blinked rapidly a few times. Chihuahua Morse code for yes, I figured, considering the plush pink-and-white coat with rhinestone hearts sewn on it. The sparkling collar added to the glitter. Mary put her on the floor, and the dog made her rounds greeting everyone.

The loud voice that carried down the hallway worked like a doorbell announcing the arrival of Ivan and his brother. The Professor had placed the container on the counter. Mary opened it, revealing chocolate squares decorated with walnut halves on top of chocolate icing. She took them out, and I could see a layer of white in the middle.

"Mississippi mud cake," Mary announced. "I had fun with the Southern drawl yesterday and my mind turned in the direction of a Southern treat."

The rich smell of chocolate drifted into the air.

"What's the white stuff in the middle?" Gertie asked.

Mary smiled. "Marshmallow cream. It makes a wonderful contrast to the dark chocolate."

Phil and Andy arrived and the group took a few minutes to get refreshments and chat with them. The two stopped at the inn several times a month and participated in many of the town's festivals, but the Sentinels didn't always have an opportunity to see them. Helen added drinks to the sideboard.

I heard a ping from my phone. Daniel texted he wouldn't be able to make the meeting. His tribal gathering must be taking longer than he thought it would.

"Daniel won't be able to join us," I said.

Gertie looked at the clock. "Noon, everyone."

That was the call to business. We all sat. I took a few minutes and filled Andy and Phil in on what the charts represented and why the people were listed on them.

Gertie pulled out her notepad, picked up her pen, and gazed expectantly around at the group. "I've added what we discussed last night. Does anyone have new information?"

I shared with them what I knew about Clarence's food as well as the theft of the sinker log and Daniel's emergency meeting. Rudy added the information to the charts.

"Timothy's been in touch," the Professor said. "Clarence is continuing to improve. He's hoping he'll be released tomorrow. Timothy asked him again if he put any mushrooms in his food, given he was so confused last night. Clarence said he definitely didn't add anything."

Rudy stood and put *how* after the word *poisoned* on Clarence's chart.

"I have more to add," I said reluctantly, knowing they would worry. I told them about my unplanned dip in the river and the threatening note.

Mary's rosy cheeks paled. "Kelly, it sounds like you're in danger. Maybe you should sit this investigation out."

"No way. Daniel needs all the help he can get. And the note is only a threat. It doesn't mean someone is really going to do something."

"But someone did," Rudy said.

"We don't know what happened, and I'm still here. One of the suspects actually saved me. If he had wanted me dead, there's a good chance I wouldn't be here. Would any of you back out if you were in my place?"

Their silence gave the answer.

Yet again, I promised to be careful.

The Professor cleared his throat. "Well then, let's get busy and complete this investigation."

"Yah," Ivan rumbled. He placed his work-weathered hands, now clenched into fists, on the table. "Need to find murderer."

I turned to Phil and Andy. "Did you hear or see anything last night you think might be helpful?"

Andy shook his head. "I wish I could say yes. The group last night included some locals, but most of them were from out of town. People will drive long distances to attend one of Roger's parties. Many of them were from the Bay Area. They're more than happy to pay for a hotel room and spend the night."

"It started in his gallery," Phil said. "Then, after an hour, everyone moved up the hill to the main house."

Phil rose and went to the sideboard. "The man has class. There were covered golf carts driven by the valets he'd hired to shuttle people up and down the hill."

"I prepared the cheese trays in the main kitchen and his staff took them to the gallery," Andy added.

Phil returned to his seat with his plate replenished with a variety of cheeses and crackers. "I didn't hear anyone talking about the murder. It's not like they aren't a gossiping group, it's just the subject of discussion was more likely to be who's cheating on whom or whether or not the watch so-and-so was wearing was a knockoff or the real thing."

Andy nodded. "I didn't hear any mention of murder."

"Did you see any heavy equipment?" I asked.

"Like what?" Andy asked.

I shrugged. "Maybe a crane or a tractor the size of one you might see at a construction site."

Phil shook his head. "Nothing like that. Now ask me if I saw Ferraris, Porsches, and Lamborghinis, and I'll give you a different answer."

"I understand the party tonight is for locals," Andy said. "Maybe we'll have more luck there."

I nodded. "I've been invited. Roger said the party is his thank-you to people supporting the event by offering different activities."

"We'll be much more likely to hear the local buzz," Phil said.

Ivan frowned and whispered something in Rudy's ear...or at least tried to keep his voice down. I heard him say *bees buzz*. Were the people bringing bees? I was close enough to hear Rudy's whispered answer as he explained what it meant to his brother.

"Mary, did you meet with Elise?" Gertie asked.

Mary batted her eyelashes and switched to a Southern drawl. "Well, darlin', that woman's red-hot anger when the name Ned Blaine is mentioned would melt the ice cubes in a mint julep."

"Bravo to the actress," Rudy said.

Mary sighed. "Unfortunately, it didn't get me anything new."

"If she's that angry, I think it's very personal," I said. "I believe Ned was blackmailing her or someone she cares deeply about."

"There's her son and her mother," Gertie said. "I'm not aware of any other family."

"Do you know if she's dating anyone?" Rudy asked.

"She was alone at the last couple of functions where I saw her," Mary replied.

Rudy added notes to the charts.

"Mr. Mushroom called," the Professor said. "He didn't have anything new about Ned Blaine. However, the Fungi Finders discovered an area on federal land where someone is cutting down redwoods and hauling them out. It's a criminal offense."

"Are the trees worth risking that?" I asked.

The Professor nodded. "Oh, yes. They can bring in thousands of dollars."

Rudy wrote the information on the "other" chart.

Mary frowned. "Maybe we can work on that when we're finished with this case. It's a pity for future generations to lose their redwoods."

The Professor's phone played a classical tune. "It's Timothy." He stepped into the hallway.

Rather than being able to remove suspects and cross questions off, we just kept adding to the charts. It felt like Ned Blaine's killer was drifting farther away.

The Professor returned. "We have new information." He looked at me. "It seems Clarence became a little too caught up in the contest." He paused. "Turns out he followed you and Daniel when you went mushroom hunting Thursday afternoon. He went back to the area that evening."

"But that's the night Ned Blaine was killed...and the place where he was shot," I said.

"I know," said the Professor.

Had Clarence seen something? Did the killer want him silenced?

Was someone trying to murder Clarence?

Chapter 21

A chorus of questions and comments collided in chaotic confusion. Mary's "Oh, my!" got lost in Ivan's "Ha!"

"Did he see anything?" I asked.

At the same time, Gertie declared, "I'm disappointed in that young man."

Rudy opened his mouth, but the Professor beat him to it. "Calm down, everyone. He didn't see anything relating to Ned Blaine's murder." He turned to Gertie. "And he's very embarrassed and apologetic. The more he thought about it, the more he realized how wrong he'd been to follow Kelly and Daniel. He'd, in essence, been spying on them. He decided that night he wouldn't go there during the contest."

"He needs to tell Deputy Sheriff Stanton," Gertie said.

"Timothy said he's already called him."

"Good," I said. "Maybe the police can help him remember something he saw or heard that's important."

Rudy went to the chart and added what we'd just learned.

I looked at Clarence's information. "Maybe someone thinks he saw something, and hence the poisonous mushrooms."

I shook my head. Still more questions instead of answers.

Gertie's pen was poised. "Okay, group. Next steps?"

The Professor said, "I have the names of the mushroom hunters who found the logged area. I'll go talk to them to see if they have anything to add. I'll swing by the hospital and talk to Clarence as well."

Mary frowned and picked up a piece of cake. She nibbled on it. "I can think up some questions for Elise and make another attempt to get information from her."

Andy and Phil said they'd continue to watch and listen at the party. Ivan and Rudy had a lead on some people selling legal sinker wood they would talk to. Gertie promised to continue questioning her garden group but wasn't optimistic about finding out anything important.

Our next steps sounded like we were close to standing still.

A rapid knock on the door was a welcome interruption to our meager plan. "Come in," I said.

Tommy opened the door and held up a clear plastic bag. "I brought cookies for Mary."

I saw the pink glitter and the Chihuahua form I'd seen earlier. Fred pushed in behind Tommy and trotted to where Princess had curled up on the floor. She jumped up, and they did a little "hello" doggie dance, their nails clicking on the hardwood floor.

Tommy went to Mary and handed her the treats. "I thought you might like these. I made some that look like Fred, and I didn't want his friend Princess to feel bad."

Mary's eyes were wide as she gazed at the creations. "Tommy, these are precious. Thank you so much."

She pulled him into her ample bosom and gave him a hug. His face turned almost as pink as the sweater Princess was wearing.

"Gotta go." He and Fred left at their usual fast pace.

I leaned back in my chair. "I'll be seeing Deputy Stanton this afternoon. Maybe he'll have something to add."

We agreed to meet at eight the next morning. Phil and Andy had appointments and wouldn't be able to attend. They promised they'd text. Gertie adjourned the meeting. Mary packed Princess in her doggie purse and put Tommy's cookies in with her cake.

"I'll be driving Mary home. Does anyone else need a ride?" the Professor asked.

"I'd appreciate one," Gertie said. "A neighbor drove me. Your offer will save him a trip."

The others declined. Everyone gathered his or her belongings and departed, each with their next role to play in the hunt for Ned Blaine's killer.

I picked up the food tray and took it to the kitchen. Helen was stirring ingredients in a bowl next to the mixer.

She stopped when I entered, and took the tray from me. "I'll take care of this, Kelly."

"Okay. Thanks."

Elise was sitting at the counter putting her knives in their case, her shoulders slumped and her movements slow. She wore a pilling navy sweater and wrinkled tan slacks.

"Hi, Elise." Concerned, I added, "How are you doing?"

She gave me a half-hearted smile. "Fine, thanks."

Her weary tone belied her words.

"I heard lots of positive comments about your class." I hoped she'd open up to what was going on.

"That's nice to know," came her tired response.

Something was seriously bothering her. "What's next for you?"

"I'll be stepping in as a substitute cook at a local grill while the regular guy is on vacation. After that...I don't know. Something will come along." She tied her knife roll and stood.

The upbeat mushroom teacher had been replaced by a downhearted woman without a full-time job. The class had provided a spark in her pocketbook, but not a long-lasting flame of support. This was a difficult time for her. I felt sorry about what she was going through.

"The man who got sick last night is going to be okay," I said.

"Thanks for telling me. I checked with the hospital, but they wouldn't tell me much except he was out of intensive care."

"Deputy Stanton was here when he got your message about the salad. He took the food to a lab."

Elise shook her head. "I have no idea how those mushrooms got in there."

Helen wrapped the remaining cheese in plastic wrap and put it in the refrigerator. She paused a moment, then took out a container. "Kelly, do you know what this is? It's labeled *Max*."

I recognized it as one of the plastic boxes Clarence kept for dog treats. I put it on the counter, opened it, and saw a piece of chicken and some cream sauce with mushrooms in it.

"It looks like Clarence was planning to give this to his dog, Max."

Elise came over and slid the leftovers toward her. "People food can be bad for dogs. Maybe Clarence didn't know that. This particular dish is very rich. I'll throw the chicken in the garbage bag and wash the container. It's the least I can do for him."

I reached out and pulled the box back. "This is something Clarence ate, and it has mushrooms in it. I'll give it to Deputy Stanton."

Elise grabbed the side of the container, rolled her eyes, and laughed. "Of course it has mushrooms. It was a mushroom-themed dinner. This is something I made. No one put poisonous mushrooms in it. It's time to toss it."

I kept a tight hold on the food. "You don't know that for sure. You didn't know someone put something in the salad."

Elise kept her grip on the container. We did what my brothers called a hard stare. Neither of us talked or moved for several seconds…we just stared at each other.

She released her hold and shrugged. "Whatever. Go ahead and waste the county's money on an unnecessary lab test." Elise put her knives in her box of tools and picked it up, along with a plastic bag. "I still have some food to get out of the refrigerators in your shed, then I'll be leaving."

Elise left. I wondered what the push-pull war of wills had been about. Helen was busy with the next steps in her recipe and didn't appear to have seen the exchange.

The inn's phone rang, and Helen answered it. She listened for a moment then shot me a worried look. "Of course she can stay with us, Daniel." She hung up.

"What's up?"

"Daniel's been asked to come in to answer more questions, by a policeman other than Bill. He asked if Allie could stay here while he was gone…and overnight if he's arrested."

Shocked, I said, "Arrested? Any idea what made him think that might happen?"

Helen shook her head. She began wringing the red-checked dish towel she held in her hands. "He didn't say. I'll get some milk and cookies ready for Allie. Tommy's running some errands, so that will give her some time to settle in."

Helen pulled out the jar of freshly made chocolate chip cookies she always kept ready for the guests and poured a big glass of milk.

I thought about Daniel's work responsibilities but wasn't worried about Ridley House. I knew Daniel's staff could handle what needed to be done. If there was a problem, they'd contact me. I *was* worried about this new turn of events and Daniel's concern he might not make it back tonight.

I pulled out one of the order folders to check our supplies but couldn't concentrate. It wasn't long before I heard Daniel's bus pass by the side window. I went to the back door. He parked in back, and he and Allie got out. She stood in front of him with a backpack in her hand.

Daniel put both hands on her shoulders. I couldn't hear what he said, but I saw her stand a little straighter and thrust her chin out. Suddenly she dropped her bag and wrapped her arms around her father's waist. Tears poured down her face, and her shoulders heaved up and down.

Her pain and fear stabbed at my heart.

He stroked her hair. Then he gently pulled her arms away and gave her a big hug. Daniel went to the bus and pulled out a box of tissues. She took a couple, wiped her eyes, and picked up her backpack.

I could read his lips as he said, "I've got to go, Allie. It's important I'm not late."

They hugged again.

She trudged up the back steps.

I opened the back door and greeted her. "Hi, Allie. Come on in."

Daniel waited while she entered. As she came in, I heard Daniel say, "I plan on seeing you tonight, Allie."

The question is will he see her in his thoughts, his dreams, or in person?

He waved, got in his vehicle, and drove off.

Allie's lips quivered. Helen went to her and gave her a hug.

Allie's lips trembled more and tears began to well up in her eyes.

Helen had put the cookies and milk on a tray. "I made you a snack. Why don't you go over by the stove and the beanbag chairs? Tommy will be back in a little bit."

Allie didn't budge. "Dad had me pack overnight things." She stopped talking.

Helen and I waited in silence.

Then Allie said, "In case he doesn't come back."

I stepped toward her. "Allie, that's not going to happen. He didn't do anything wrong."

"My mom left without saying a word. Just left a note saying family life didn't suit her. Now I could lose my dad."

She stumbled to the counter, dropped her bag, sat down, and buried her head in her arms. Sobs wracked her slim body. Her long, straight black hair covered her face. After a couple of minutes, her crying began to slow.

Michael. Why hadn't I thought of him earlier?

I went and stood next to her, lightly touching her shoulder. "Allie, your dad has a very wealthy, influential man behind him."

She brought her head up out of her arms. Her eyes were red and swollen. Her wet cheeks glistened from the flood of tears.

"Who?" she whispered.

"Michael Corrigan, the owner of Resorts International and the man who hired your dad."

"Why would he help?" She struggled to talk through her constricted throat.

I could barely make out her words. "Because he's that kind of man. He considers the people who work for him a family...and it's his nature to help people. That's why he built the community center."

For the first time, I saw a glimmer of hope in her eyes.

"I'll call him right now and tell him what's going on. And I'll text your dad about what I'm doing."

Allie sat a little straighter. Helen had quietly placed tissues next to her. She took a few and wiped her eyes and face.

"Thank you." Her voice still trembled, but the words were stronger.

Helen picked up Allie's bag. "I'll put this in the corner by the door. That way you'll remember it when you go home tonight."

Allie gave her a feeble smile.

"Now, how about some milk and cookies?"

I remembered Helen mentioning Allie buying horse books at the fair. "Do you like horses?"

Allie nodded.

"I have a new copy of *Today's Horseman*. I'll get that for you."

Helen got her settled next to the stove. It supplied most of the heat for the room, and we kept it going throughout the day most of the time. I retrieved the magazine and gave it to Allie, and she began flipping through the pages.

I went back to my room and called Michael. I got a recording and left a brief message about what had happened. I knew he'd put wheels in motion as soon as he heard it.

Anger seared through me. I clenched my fists. We'd work this out, but the pain and angst it was causing now made me furious.

I knew one person who could give me information.

I was going to find out who Ned Blaine was blackmailing.

Elise was going to tell me.

Chapter 22

I marched through the kitchen. Helen and Allie were on the couch looking at the magazine together. I was glad they couldn't see my face. I was on the warpath and was sure it showed.

A whirlwind of emotion engulfed me as I stormed across the parking lot. The cool ocean breeze did nothing to soothe my roiling emotions. I flung open the door of the storage shed.

Elise was filling a large cooler with the contents from one of the refrigerators. She turned, looked at me, and stopped what she was doing. Her eyes widened. She closed the lid of the chest.

My arms were ramrod straight at my sides, my hands balled into fists. "You're going to tell me who Ned Blaine was blackmailing."

Her eyes narrowed. "And why am I going to do that?"

"Because if you don't, I'm going to call Deputy Sheriff Stanton now and tell him what you and Joey gave him for Joey's Thursday night alibi isn't true. It was a lie."

Elise looked startled. "What are you talking about? He was watching the basketball game with his friends, just like we said."

"That might have been what he told you, but that isn't the case."

"How do you know that?"

"I went on the tour with him yesterday. During the time the people were hunting for mushrooms, I stayed with him and the other drivers. One of them said he missed a good game. Joey replied a job came up he needed to do."

Elise sat abruptly in a nearby chair. She had a panicked look on her face.

"So, who was Ned blackmailing?" I took a step toward her. "I know you know. You said to me the person you're protecting didn't kill Ned."

Her panic turned to fear. Elise's gaze darted around the room as if she was searching for a way out.

I kept pushing. "When the police find out who Ned targeted, it's going to look bad for you and whoever his blackmail victim was for not coming forward. It shouts you're trying to hide what Ned was doing."

"What the person was being blackmailed about wasn't worth killing someone to hide it."

"All the more reason for you to come forward."

She stood and lifted the lid to the ice chest and began rearranging its contents. "It could still mean jail time."

"Sounds like you're not even sure that would happen. It would be unfortunate if withholding information caused the person to become a serious suspect in a murder investigation."

"Why do you care so much?"

"There's a young girl crying her eyes out because her father is a suspect in Ned's murder, and he's being questioned. I'm not letting this go."

Elise slammed the lid down. "All right. Ned was blackmailing my son."

The Silver Sentinels and I were correct about it being someone close to her. "Why?"

"Someone hired him to retrieve sinker logs. He doesn't have a permit. Tried but couldn't get one."

"Who was he working for?"

"I don't know. He didn't tell me, and I didn't ask."

"How did Ned Blaine find out?"

"Secretly following him, like he did with everyone else." She pulled a second ice chest up next to the refrigerator and opened the lid. She began taking out food and tossing it helter-skelter into the cooler. "For Pete's sake. It's old wood. Who cares what happens to it. It gave us some extra money."

She glared at me. If the daggers in her eyes had been real, I'd have joined Ned Blaine by now.

"What did Ned want?"

"At first he asked for money, but Joey didn't have any. He gave me any he didn't need for living expenses. Like I said before, a good son helping out." Elise stopped talking and continued cleaning out the refrigerator. An unopened brick of cheese followed a red-lidded container of butter.

"So then what happened?"

She straightened. "When the money wasn't forthcoming, he demanded to know who Joey was working for." Elise went back to filling the ice chest.

"Then what?" My gritted teeth made the words curt and abrupt.

"He finally told Ned. The person wasn't doing the actual stealing. He could say he didn't know it was stolen. Probably the worst that would happen would be a fine and the wood confiscated. Joey's the one who needed to worry about possible jail time."

Made sense. I knew Roger fit that description. But he'd also said he'd lost out to Asian buyers on occasion.

Joey wasn't off the suspect list of murderers yet. But if what Elise said was true, he'd committed no major crime and was trying to help out in a situation of strapped finances. He wasn't being blackmailed for something serious.

"You need to tell the police. Better yet, you and Joey should do it together. You can explain the circumstances. It'll look better for you, and they might go easier on both of you. I'll give you a chance to do that."

Elise returned to the chair and slumped against the workbench next to it. She ran her fingers through her hair. "Joey's never been in trouble. If the police find out he lied about the alibi and Ned was blackmailing him, it will look really bad. But you're right. We need to tell them."

"You have until six this evening to go to the police on your own. After that, I'll tell them myself." I started to leave, then turned back. "By the way, what was with the container tug-of-war in the kitchen earlier?"

"I don't know what you mean. It was a very rich recipe and bad for dogs to eat. Why is it I offer to do something nice and you twist it into something else?"

I felt there was more to it than that, but I didn't think I was going to find out. I said no more and left. When I got back to the kitchen, Helen told me Michael Corrigan had returned my call.

I called him and felt a surge of energy at hearing his voice. He was a big, burly, strong man and his voice vibrated with life.

"Hi, Kelly. Thanks for letting me know about what's happening. I contacted a San Francisco law firm I deal with and they're sending an attorney. I've arranged to have him flown to Redwood Cove. One of the veterans from the center will pick him up and drive him to the police station. The company has already put in motion what we'll need to do to post bail if it comes to that."

"Thanks, Michael. His daughter is really hurting."

"Understandable. We'll get him home."

"I'll let him know."

I texted Daniel about what was happening as soon as I got off the phone.

I returned to the work area. Tommy had gotten back and he and Allie were flipping through the magazine, putting sticky notes on some of the pages. Fred's head rested on Tommy's feet.

"What are you two up to?"

"Choosing which horses we like best," Tommy said.

This was a nice safe conversation. Continuing it for a bit seemed like a good idea. "Show me which ones you've picked."

Allie flipped to a photo of a leopard Appaloosa.

"Would you like to see a horse like that in person?" I asked.

She nodded enthusiastically.

"I can take you next weekend if you like. His name is Nezi."

"Cool," she said.

"Can I come, too?" Tommy asked.

"Yes, but Fred will have to stay home. Dogs, other than the ranch dogs, aren't allowed on the property."

"That's okay. He understands he can't always come with me."

Tommy slid down on the floor and gave Fred a hug. He picked up a rope toy, and they began pulling each other from side to side. I looked at Allie and inclined my head toward the kitchen.

A cloud passed over her face as she followed me. We sat at the kitchen counter and I said, "Like I told you, the man who I said would help is doing exactly that. You and your dad aren't alone in this. Now you have a very powerful person working on your behalf. In addition, there's also a whole group of people, including myself, searching for answers."

I told her what was happening.

Relief brightened her face. "Wow! Thank you so much."

She rejoined Tommy, only this time with a smile on her face.

Helen took tomorrow morning's breakfast pastries out of the oven and put them on cooling racks. I could see orange flecks on the top and knew they were one of my favorites—orange muffins. Their rich smell, combined with the fire's warmth, gave the area a cozy, comforting, feeling…a good thing for Allie right now.

"Tommy met Priscilla the pig this morning and wants to go back into town to see her again. He got to pet her, and she did a little dance. Allie wants to see her, too." Helen took off her apron. "His owner said he'd be giving her a break at two thirty."

"That'll be a good distraction for Allie," I said.

I caught Helen up on the part Michael Corrigan was playing on Daniel's behalf. Now she was the one with a look of relief on her face.

"We won't be there long," Helen said. "I'll be back in time to put out the wine and appetizers."

She gathered up the kids, and I checked the afternoon list of events. Time to talk to Joey. I called the off-roading company.

A man answered. "Hello, Happy Trails Off-Roading Company."

"Do you have any space available in the three o'clock mushroom-hunting group?"

"We sure do. We just had a cancellation. I'd be happy to sign you up."

Sometimes the opposite of Murphy's Law was at work. I was about to say *great* and give him my name, but then I had second thoughts.

"I'm still making up my mind. I'll get back to you."

"Okay." He hung up.

It had occurred to me going off with Joey and his friends wasn't exactly being extra careful, like I'd promised. The mushroom hunters would be off in the woods, and I'd be alone with them. Add to that my plan to question Joey...and I needed to think of another plan.

Maybe I could ask Scott if he wanted to go with me. Then I reconsidered. Not a good idea. Scott wasn't happy about the investigating I was involved in.

I looked at the contest flyer. A break was scheduled at the meeting area near the town square before the last group went out. I'd go try to see if I could talk to Joey then.

There was a little time before I had to leave and I picked up the work folder again. This time I could concentrate, and the numbers made sense. I hoped Deputy Stanton arrived before I had to go, in case he'd learned something he could share with me. As if on cue, he rolled into the parking lot. Once again I waved him in.

He sat next to me at the counter. I couldn't tell if it was his massive leather belt carrying the tools of his trade creaking, or him. The lines in his face seemed much deeper than they had this morning.

"Coffee?" I asked.

He nodded. "Thanks."

I filled a mug and put it in front of him. He put his hands around it and seemed to let the warmth of the cup seep into him. He took a sip.

"Have the cookies helped you through the day at all?"

Stanton gave a tired chuckle. "Yes. As much for their taste as the smile they brought when I looked at them. Happiness is a commodity I don't have much of in my line of work." He took out his notepad and a pen. "So, tell me what you know and show me the note."

I was surprised at how much there was to share with him. The threatening message on the car, the stolen sinker log, the plunge in the river, and the

Fungi Finders with their discovery of the illegal logging, all combined to make quite a list. I kept my word to Elise. I'd give her time to help herself and Joey out. I went and got the note.

"You've had quite the day, and it's only midafternoon," Stanton said. "I wonder what else you're going to uncover before it's over."

I wondered, too.

"I'll talk to the canoe guides. If they know anything, I think they'll tell me. I've helped a couple of them out of some scrapes from too much boneheaded teenage energy when they were younger." He stared at the message with the glued letters. "Kelly, the note and the shove into the river are serious."

"I know. I'll continue to be vigilant and not do anything reckless."

Stanton stretched. "I can understand why you thought you were safe with the guides around...but you weren't."

I hated to say it, but he was right. "I know. I'll be extra careful."

It was the second time today I'd made that promise.

He put the note in a baggie. "I'll take this in, but I doubt we'll learn anything. I heard about the redwoods being cut down and the sinker log. I spoke with Clarence, and it doesn't seem like he saw anything. No vehicles or people. Quite the red face about following you and Daniel."

I went to the refrigerator and retrieved what had been intended as a treat for Max. "Helen found this, and it has some mushrooms in it. I believe it was part of Clarence's meal."

I gave it to him and described my encounter with Elise. I'd keep my word about the blackmailing, but I had no desire to shield the woman any further. It probably meant nothing, but I wanted Stanton to know.

"It makes sense to check it out. I'll take it and drop it off with the same person who's analyzed the mushrooms in the salad."

"Did you find out anything about the mushrooms in it?"

"Definitely poisonous. The doc at the dinner was right about the type it was." He stood. "I heard about Daniel going in for more questioning. For the record, I think he's innocent."

"I'm glad to hear that."

"Ned overstepped the line grabbing Allie's arm, but Daniel doesn't have a volatile temper. He's thoughtful and deliberate. He gave his message to Blaine, and according to him that was the end of it. I believe him."

We said our good-byes. I glanced at the clock.

Time to confront Joey.

He shook his head. "I have my reasons for not saying. I'll tell the police, not you." He looked at his hands, took out a pocketknife, and began cleaning under his nails.

I paused. "Your mom told me you gave Blaine the name of the person who hired you. Who was it?"

"I agreed with Mom we'll talk to the police when the next tour ends... and I will. There's no reason for me to tell you."

Frustrated, I realized I'd used my leverage regarding his alibi on Elise. The only other thing I knew about him was what Roger had told me.

"I know you and Peter sold sinker logs to Roger Simmons."

Joey shrugged. "The ones Simmons told you about were legal. There are still some of those available."

I suspected Roger was the one who had hired Joey and probably Peter to retrieve the illegal ones, but Joey had balked at giving me that information. I didn't know if finding out about the legal ones would help, but I decided to ask anyway.

"Where did they come from?"

He eyed me for a moment. "Peter inherited them. An uncle died recently and left him his farm. He found dried sinker logs in a barn on the property. Nothing illegal about it."

"I asked Peter if he knew where I could see some. He said no."

Another shrug. "Didn't want word to get out. They're valuable and someone might steal them. So...keep it to yourself. I told you because I hoped some information might shut you up."

"Who—"

Joey interrupted me. "Listen, now that they have a more exact time of death and I know I can cover myself, I have some other info that might gain me some points." He smirked at me. "I'm the one who found Ned's body and called it in."

That caught me off guard. "What!"

"Yeah. I happened to go to where he was shot Friday morning. One of the guys said there were a lot of mushrooms there and we might want to take our hunters to that spot. He was right about the mushrooms, but the area wouldn't have given the people much flavor for what off-roading was like, which was part of what we wanted to have happen. We decided not to use it."

"Why didn't you tell the police right away?"

"Yeah, right. With Blaine blackmailing me. When they first questioned me, I didn't have an alibi for the whole time they wanted to know about."

"Why did you call it in?"

He put his knife away. "Didn't feel right leaving his body there. Some animal probably would've found it. I didn't like the guy, but I wouldn't wish that on anyone."

"It was thoughtful of you to do that." I paused. "It sounds like there were illegal sinker logs as well. Who were you working with?"

"That's all you're getting from me, Ms. Jackson."

I tried another tack. "Did you take the big sinker log last night? Were you driving over your tracks this morning to cover them up?"

The cold stare he gave me reminded me of the frigid water he'd pulled me from. I wondered if he was wishing he'd left me there.

"Like I said. That's. All. You're. Getting. From. Me."

Each word staccato and final. He stood. Our meeting was over.

"Thank you for your time," I said, although I doubted he heard me as he was already on his way back to his truck.

I couldn't thank him for the information he'd shared. It hadn't gotten me any closer to Ned Blaine's killer. He joined his group without another word to me.

My watch indicated it was about time for the last session to begin. I walked back toward Priscilla's fan club and saw Ted leading her away.

Tommy was waving. "Bye, Priscilla, see you tomorrow."

Her tail seemed to give an extra spin.

"Okay, kids. Let's get back to the inn," Helen said.

"I'll see you back there." I returned to the pickup. There wasn't enough room in the truck, or I would've offered them a ride back. It was a single seater, not a monster like Joey's.

I drove back with the wheels in my mind spinning much faster than those on the little pickup. I entered the inn and went straight to the conference room.

Turning on a light, I sat at the table facing the charts. What had I learned this afternoon?

I looked at the "why people kill" list. *Anger* was at the top with *fear*, *hatred*, and *revenge* as subcategories under it. Blackmailing, lying to the police, possible jail time, and stealing—all things I'd dealt with today and all capable of summoning the emotions listed. People were losing income as the location of valuable mushroom patches were sold to the public. Another reason to be angry.

From Elise's look, it was clear she hadn't realized Joey had lied about his alibi. He said he had one, but it wasn't what he told the police. I wondered what his reason was for not revealing it.

Elise mentioned Joey getting illegal logs for someone. She said the person he was selling it to wouldn't be in serious trouble, so he'd given the name to Ned. Joey had specifically said the ones Roger bought and told me about were legal. Maybe Roger had paid Joey and Peter to retrieve illegal ones, too. Technically he wouldn't be buying those. Joey's wording wouldn't have been a lie. Joey was better with words than I thought.

Most likely it was Roger who hired them. But Elise was right about not seeing any motive for murder there. If Roger wanted to, he could buy the local paper and fire Blaine. That would have given Ned something to worry about and gotten him out of Roger's hair if he'd been bothering him.

Who took the big sinker log and who had it? My best guess was Joey and Peter took it, with Roger providing the funds for the equipment. It might have been one of the Asian buyers he mentioned, but, for now, I was sticking with the suspects we had.

Who else could Ned have been blackmailing? Roger? All the reasons for the threat not being a big deal applied here...unless there was something else Roger had to hide. There was no indication of that so far. The destruction of the federal land might hold more consequences. But Ned couldn't have blackmailed him about that because the reporter was already dead when that happened.

Ned was killed near where the stolen sinker log had been. Seemed like a big coincidence, but what kind of connection could there be with the reporter being murdered before the theft?

I looked at Clarence's chart. The man of many laughs. Now we had an idea why someone might want to kill him. He said he hadn't seen anything, but the killer didn't necessarily know that. In which case, the murderer might have been at the dinner. Back to the four suspects. They'd all been there, walking around in the kitchen.

I'd been focusing on the logs. Now I looked at the mushroom chart.

The only smoking lead there, so far, was Peter's fiery temper. Other people were upset, but he was the only one we knew of who threatened the reporter. The Fungi Finders had felt targeted, and they wanted their information off of the website. Maybe one of them had confronted Ned.

The sacred classification for Daniel's tribe was the next chart. Initially he'd said some people were mad, but there was no indication they took action. Daniel and I hadn't had a chance to talk about it any further.

The chart labeled "other" had the illegal logging of the live redwoods on it. I couldn't see any way that fit in. It just hung out there by itself.

Elise's name was there...an angry, protective woman. I thought she could kill for any of the top emotions listed.

Who had pushed me in the water?

Who had left the threatening note?

My brain felt like the butter we made on the ranch with Grandma's wooden churn. Only, in my case, it'd been left in the sun and was beginning to melt.

My cell phone rang. I recognized Stanton's number.

"Hello."

"Wanted to let you know about the mushrooms you gave me this afternoon. Based on a visual identification, the lab said what was in his dinner was poisonous. They said there were two types of mushrooms given to Clarence. If he'd ingested just one, the amount he was given would've only made him sick. The combination of the two together almost killed him. As soon as we have a definite analysis on the second one, we'll be considering what happened to Clarence as attempted murder."

Chapter 24

I thanked Deputy Stanton for the information. Determined to keep my word to Elise, I didn't say anything about Joey. I ended the call and returned to the charts. I added "two types of poisonous mushrooms" on Clarence's chart and "attempted murder" with a question mark.

If he'd only had one type of mushroom, he would've been sick but not nearly died. Had two different people tried to make him sick but not kill him? Or had one person tried to murder him and, for some reason, used two different types of mushrooms?

I couldn't see anywhere else I could go with the information. I went to the work area to continue with the order I'd started earlier. Allie and Tommy, each curled up on a beanbag chair, were reading paperback books. I saw a horse and foal on Allie's cover and a long-eared dog that looked a lot like Fred on Tommy's. Fred rested his head on the boy's shoulder, as though he was reading along with him.

Helen was putting plates and silverware on a tray. She signaled me over. "Any news of Daniel?" she whispered.

I shook my head. "We should hear soon. Unless something went wrong, the attorney ought to be with Daniel by now. I'll let you know as soon as I learn something."

She nodded. I went back to the folder I'd left on the worktable. I'd just opened it to figure out where I left off when I heard a vehicle in the driveway. A familiar faded blue van rattled by.

Daniel!

I started to say something but decided to let Daniel do the surprising.

He opened the door and strode in.

Allie looked up. "Dad!" she screamed and ran to him, again flinging her arms around him, only this time from happiness, not fear.

He hugged her tightly. "I love you."

Helen and I both were wiping tears from the corners of our eyes.

Allie stepped back, beaming at her father. Then she spun around and raced toward me. The next thing I knew I was the recipient of an around-the-waist hug.

"Thank you! Thank you! Thank you!" she said.

Fred began baying, which brought some comic relief to the emotional scene. Tommy looked perplexed. I didn't know if he knew anything about what had been happening with Allie's father.

"Everyone's happy to see you, including Fred," I said to Daniel.

"And I'm happy to see all of you. Kelly, thank you for your quick thinking about calling Michael."

"You're welcome. I wish I'd thought of it sooner."

Helen came up to him and touched his arm. "I'm so glad you're back."

"Thanks," he said with a big grin. "I was thinking takeout from Sam's Deli tonight. Are you and Tommy in?"

"Sounds perfect," Helen replied.

"Kelly, how about you?"

"I'll have to pass. I'm attending a party tonight for people and businesses that supported the mushroom-hunting contest."

Daniel put his arm around Allie's shoulders. "I want to talk to Kelly for a few minutes. Why don't you and Tommy get the deli menu and decide what you'd like tonight."

"Okay, Dad."

The kids raced each other to where the takeout menus were kept in the cupboard. When they had an even start, Allie always won with her long legs. As she grabbed the food list, Tommy ran back to where they'd been sitting. With his head start, it was a tie.

"Let's go into the conference room," I said to Daniel.

He nodded and followed me, then whistled when he saw the charts and everything written on them. "You and the Silver Sentinels have been busy."

"We've learned a lot…just not who the murderer is yet," I said ruefully.

"What's the bit about a note and being shoved into the river?"

I explained, being as brief as I could, to keep his concern as minimal as possible.

He raised his eyebrows at me.

"I know, I know. Be careful," I said in response to his look. "Is there any information you can add to our investigation?"

"Not really. The tribal meeting was about restoring the land. It'll be expensive. The police only asked questions. They didn't tell me anything I didn't already know."

"What happened when the attorney arrived?"

"The whole tone changed as soon as he got there." He gave me one of his sheepish grins. "I guess it was pretty silly of me to think the fact I was innocent was all I needed and my honesty would get me through this."

"No, Daniel, you weren't silly. You trust people and extend that characteristic to others. You believe the police will get to the truth."

"I was pretty tense by the time help arrived. Three officers questioned me. There wasn't a friendly look from any of them."

"If it's any comfort to you, Deputy Stanton thinks you're innocent."

"Thanks. It does help."

We joined the others. The clock said five thirty. I'd be late for the party, but Roger had said it was a buffet and to stop by anytime. I excused myself and went to change.

A Redwood Cove party. With Daniel home, I could get more in the mood for one, even though the situation wasn't resolved. Casual was the usual theme. I chose an emerald green sweater—one my sister said did wonders for my green eyes. She always thought about clothes and makeup, the opposite of me. Black jeans and black leather flats finished the look.

I traded my everyday gold posts for diamond ones, a gift from my mom. I decided to put on some eye shadow but stopped mid–makeup application when I realized I hadn't spent this much time thinking about what I looked like in a long while.

Scott was going to be there tonight.

Was this for him?

I swallowed hard and pushed the thought away, my stomach still clenching when I remembered the pain I'd been through from my divorce. Over the years I'd encouraged friends and family to heal and leave behind their emotional wounds. Maybe it was time for me to take my own advice.

I willed myself to stop thinking about Scott and finished getting ready. Helen was alone in the kitchen when I entered.

"You look lovely, Kelly. Those earrings match the sparkle in your eyes."

"It's so wonderful having Daniel back. It's put me in a party mood."

Helen put the finishing touches on a cheese tray. "I know what you mean. I'm sure we'll all be happy when this is cleared up."

"I agree. Maybe I'll learn something tonight," I said as I left. I decided to take my down jacket. Northern California nights are normally quite cold. I got into the truck and headed for Roger's place.

I drove up the long driveway. The outside lights were on at the studio. I stopped out of their range. Should I try to see if the sinker log was in the work area? I looked behind me and saw no headlights from approaching cars. I'd promised to be careful. It would only take me a few minutes, and no one was coming up the hill.

I retrieved my flashlight from the glove box and got out. The wind tossed my hair around and strands stung my cheeks. The thunderous sound of crashing waves, as well as moist ocean air against my face, reminded me of the nearby sea.

I looked down the drive again. Still no headlights. I kept the building between myself and the main house, so my light wouldn't be seen, and turned on the flashlight, carefully checking for motion detector lights. We had them at the ranch to discourage predators, so I was familiar with them. Seeing none, and not finding any surveillance cameras, I looked down the driveway again. Still clear of approaching vehicle headlights.

I kept the light low and went around the side of the structure and up to a window. Darn! It was covered by a shade, and I noticed bars on the inside. I went back to the front and checked for anyone coming up the road. Still clear. There were advantages to being late.

I went to the back of the building to check for equipment. Nothing. The ground provided no tire prints because it was concrete. There were two large barn-size doors to allow equipment to enter, but they were secured with a heavy chain and padlock. No way in there and no windows to see through.

I hurried back to my car and continued up the hill. I hadn't learned anything, but I was glad I had tried. A valet greeted me. I recognized him as one of the men I'd seen in the field at the community center.

"Hi," I said. "I'm Kelly Jackson. I saw you working with one of the PTSD dogs Friday night. Are you enjoying it?"

"Totally. Zeus is a great dog. On one hand, it's going to be hard to give him up. On the other, he's going to a friend of mine who's going to become a tenant at the center, so I'll still be able to see him."

"Are you going to work with another dog?"

"You bet. It's possible we'll be able to have our own personal pets in our cabins. That's under consideration. Then I'll get my own dog as well as train one for someone else."

Michael Corrigan loved dogs, and he believed they added to the well-being of people's lives. He'd arranged for employees to be able to have dogs on his properties if they passed their Canine Good Citizenship test. I suspected the veteran who wanted a dog wasn't going to have a problem having that happen.

I handed him my keys. "My guess is you'll have that chance."

He handed me a ticket, and I headed for the house. A note on the door said, *Come on in.* I did. The entryway had two large coat racks. I put my jacket on a hanger and went to join the party I could hear was well under way as the sound of happy voices floated from the room.

I walked into the crowded dining room, where an oversize table held a buffet feast. Trays of quarter-cut sandwiches followed a variety of appetizers, all neatly labeled. Phil had a wine table at the far end of it.

Andy busily arranged trays at his cheese area. A guest pointed to a wedge of dark orange cheese and I knew, from Andy's animated movements, the person was getting the history, a description of the taste, and the region it was from. He loved his cheese.

Over in the corner, Elise, Joey, and Peter were standing close together, as thick as thieves—which they might possibly be. I wondered if Peter and Elise were dating.

Roger saw me and headed in my direction. "I'm glad you could make it."

"I am, too. Thanks for the invitation."

"Let me introduce you to some people who might be helpful for you to know in terms of running the inn and advising your guests."

He proceeded to introduce me to the owner of a vegan cooking school, the head chef at a large restaurant, and the CEO of the chamber of commerce, among others. We exchanged cards and promised to get together in the near future.

"Thank you, Roger. They all seem like really nice people, and I'll be able to learn more about some of the unique offerings of this area."

"You're welcome. Enjoy the evening."

He wandered off to be the charming host to other guests. I headed for the buffet. I'd had a snack at the Silver Sentinels' meeting but no actual lunch. I filled most of my plate but left room for cheese.

Andy greeted me enthusiastically. "What delightful choice would you like today?"

"I see my favorite." I pointed to the Huntsman.

The layers of rich cheddar mingled with a blue-veined soft cheese to create a combination to delight the palate.

"Of course." He cut a slice and put it on my plate. "I'd like to recommend this nettle and jack cheese. It's a new one on my list. Would you like to try it?"

"I'm always up for what you suggest. You're the cheesemonger."

He put a couple of slices next to the Huntsman. "Enjoy."

"I'm sure I will."

I added a few crackers and found a table in a corner with an empty stool and sat. I put my purse down next to the wall. Just as I started to eat, Scott arrived, and I saw him search the room. When he saw me, his face lit up and he smiled and waved. I waved back. He came over to me.

"That looks like a wonderful selection of food." He inclined his head toward the buffet table.

"I agree. Roger did a great job of choosing an interesting variety. Why don't you grab a plate and join me?"

"I just finished dinner, so I'm not hungry. However, I'll go look at what's there. I've heard this caterer does some interesting vegan dishes. I'm always looking for new ideas."

He left, and I looked around the room, savoring my Huntsman on a wheat cracker. Elise, Peter, and Joey still were together. No mingling for them. Peter took Elise's plate and headed for the buffet. Our glances met, and he averted his eyes. I felt the same way about him. He put a few appetizers on her plate and headed back for the corner.

Scott returned and put his plate next to mine. "I thought these tempeh fries with horseradish-dill sauce looked intriguing."

They reminded me of fish sticks with tartar sauce, but I kept that to myself.

"Andy Brown gave me some of your favorite cheese—the Huntsman. The man is a very knowledgeable cheesemonger. I asked him to buy me some hard-to-find cheeses in San Francisco and bring them the next time he comes."

"He's a nice man. You two will probably have some fun cheese conversations."

"I'm sure we will." He placed a piece of cheese on a cracker. "I'm surprised Roger didn't cancel this party."

"Why is that?" I asked.

"He was gone all last night on a family emergency and didn't get back until midmorning."

As we ate, he proceeded to tell me Roger had hired two of his men who'd been acting as valets to drive him to San Francisco after the get-together last night. Roger had gotten word his aunt had had a heart attack as she was leaving the opera and was in intensive care. It was a long drive to the city with much of it on a dark, winding, two-lane road. The men had taken turns driving, while Roger tried to get some sleep in the back seat.

Roger had been making the rounds and now came up to our table.

"How is your aunt?" Scott asked. "The men told me what happened when they came back to the center to get what they needed for the trip."

"Much better. They weren't sure she was going to make it at first. My name's on the emergency contact form. I'm the one responsible for any family medical decisions that need to be made. It was important for me to be there."

"I'm glad to hear she's improving," Scott said. "The men loved the posh hotel and the two hundred dollars you said they could spend on room service for late-night snacks and breakfast."

"Happy to do it. They were excellent drivers and very conscientious about helping me. Many of the guests had left when I got the call, so it worked out for the men to leave for a while to get their belongings. I still had two other valets."

"You must be pretty tired."

"I was up all night, but I'm doing fine. I slept in the car on the way home and napped a bit this afternoon."

A young woman in a uniform came by and picked up our plates. Roger and Scott's talk turned to the next steps for the community center, and I tuned out. Roger was gone all night. That meant he couldn't have put the note on my truck, unless he did it while the drivers went to get their things. I wondered if Phil or Andy could provide more information about the evening, so I walked over to talk to them.

Andy was replenishing one of his cheese trays and Phil was surveying the room.

"I have a question about last night and Roger's trip to San Francisco," I said.

They both looked at each other, shrugged, and then Phil said, "I don't know anything about a trip."

Andy chimed in, "Neither do I."

I explained, and then Andy said, "Now I understand a comment by one of the valets. Roger hired a couple of them to come early and help us unpack. They were scheduled to help pack up at the end of last night's party as well. One of them came to me and said they had to leave for a short while to get some things from home but they'd be back in time to assist us, which they were."

"Do either of you know if Roger left while they were gone?"

"I can answer that," Phil said. "My job was to tend the wine for as long as he had company. A small number of guests lingered and Roger conversed with them from the time our helper let us know his plans until he returned. Roger was here the whole time."

"He actually left with the men before we finished packing up," Andy added. "The other valets helped us."

Roger couldn't have put the note on the window of my truck. One more small piece of the puzzle to add to our charts. The question remained, who put the threat on my truck?

Chapter 25

Roger came over to the table. "Phil, I'd like some more of the cabernet."

"Sure thing." He took Roger's glass and poured him some wine. "Roger, there are a half dozen bottles left from last night. What would you like us to do with them?"

"Please put them in the wine cellar...no, wait. Let's have a drawing and give them away to tonight's guests. They're exceptionally nice wines, worth over a hundred dollars a bottle. They'll make fun gifts."

"Great idea," Phil said.

Roger began to walk away. "I'll go cut strips of paper."

"I'd be happy to help," I volunteered.

Maybe I'll have a chance to ask him some questions.

"Wonderful. Follow me."

He led me to an enormous kitchen with black granite counters, with fluorescent blue specks embedded throughout the stone. The catering staff busily worked to replenish trays being emptied by the hungry guests. We passed through to a spacious pantry. He stopped at a series of drawers, opened one, and pulled out two orange-handled pairs of scissors. One was smaller than the other, and he handed those to me. Another drawer held plain white paper.

He took several sheets, folded them in half, and cut a few strips. "That looks about right."

Roger handed me some paper, and I began cutting. "Thanks for taking the time to introduce me to people tonight. I'm looking forward to getting together with them."

"You're welcome. I like helping local businesses, and networking is one way to do that." He opened a cabinet, pulled down a large basket, and put his paper strips in it.

I tossed mine in with his. I took a couple more sheets of paper. "Did you hear about the big sinker log being stolen?"

I sensed rather than saw a change in his demeanor. There was a tenseness that hadn't been there before.

"I did, as a matter of fact. It was a beauty. I've admired it for years."

I hesitated. I wanted to ask him if he had bought it, but that would be a clear admission on his part he'd taken in stolen property. Asking him if he took it was out of the question.

"It's probably in a cargo box on a steamer headed to China by now," Roger commented.

Or it's in your work area.

Had his attitude changed because I was asking questions about the log? Or because he was angry someone else had gotten it?

"The log was near where the reporter was killed, wasn't it?" he asked.

"Yes, his body was found on a knoll above the river in an area that looked down on where it was."

Roger cut more strips of paper. "I wonder if there's any connection."

He appeared perfectly comfortable talking about Ned Blaine's murder. I didn't sense any nervousness. If he killed Ned, he was a great actor or it seemed he didn't have any feelings about what he'd done.

"No idea," I replied. "I'll be glad when they catch whoever did it. It's scary to have a killer on the loose."

He threw more strips into the basket, and I followed suit.

Roger took another basket down from the cupboard. "The man had a lot of enemies because of all his poking around. I doubt it was a random killing. It's unlikely others are in danger."

"I hope you're right. I'll still be happy when the person is caught."

"I understand." He picked up the baskets. "We'll use the empty one for people to put their names in."

We returned to the dining area. Roger went to a credenza where a crystal pitcher sat. He picked up a matching stir stick and tapped the container with it, creating a high-pitched sound that drew people's attention. Everyone quieted.

"I have an announcement to make. We're going to have a drawing for some fine bottles of wine."

The crowd's enthusiastic response of claps, whistles, and joyful exclamations declared the idea a winner. Roger tapped again. All talking ceased.

"Kelly and I cut strips of paper for your names." He put the basket containing them on a coffee table. "I'll leave an empty one here on the credenza for you to put your slips in when you're done."

Women searched their purses for pens and men pulled them out of their shirt pockets. Roger opened a drawer in the chest, took out a tray of pens, and placed it on the coffee table. People began writing their names down and passing pens around.

I found an empty chair near the coffee table and picked up a slip of paper. The pen tray was empty. I started to rise to go get my purse, then noticed a pen was headed my way only a couple of people away. I sat and decided to wait for it.

I looked around for Scott. He was conversing with a gentleman I'd been introduced to who owned an office supply store. I figured he was doing some of his own networking.

The woman next to me tapped me on the shoulder. "Would you like a pen?"

"Yes, thanks." I took it from her.

And froze. I suddenly felt sick. I could hardly breathe.

The pen had the name of a restaurant on it. The Blue Moon Restaurant. The one that Ned said closed many years ago and claimed the pen was now one-of-a kind. It must be Ned Blaine's pen.

I felt a rush of blood to my face. It felt like I was on fire. I leaned forward, letting my hair cover the sides of my face. I put the slip on the coffee table and wrote my name. My hand shook. Without looking up, I pulled my right hand back and slipped the pen into my front jeans pocket. It was too shallow for the pen to be completely concealed, so I pulled my sweater down. It would do the job if I didn't move too much.

I took a couple of deep breaths, sat back in the chair, and scanned the room. Both Roger and Scott were staring at me. Scott had a concerned look on his face. I couldn't read Roger's expression.

Roger started toward me, as did Scott. An enthusiastic guest stepped in front of Roger, stopping him. I could hear his "thank you for the great party" from where I sat.

I stood and tugged my sweater down, went and deposited my name in the drawing basket, then wove my way through the crowd. As I retrieved my purse and headed for the entryway, I felt someone beside me.

Scott. "It's a lovely night outside. No fog and the stars are out in full force. Let's step outside for a few minutes and enjoy them."

The frown on his face made it clear this wasn't a romantic moment.

We walked out and away from the lights of the porch, then he stopped and turned to me.

"Kelly, what happened in there? You have a traffic-light face. Green is when you're smiling, yellow is the slight frown you get when you're trying to figure something out or you're concerned, and red is when you're upset. What I just saw in there was bright red. What's going on? I've never seen your face so flushed."

I unzipped my purse and pulled out a clean tissue. "I think I found Ned Blaine's pen, the reporter who was murdered."

"What are you talking about?"

As I wrapped the pen up and put it in the side pocket of my purse, I explained the pen's history.

"Someone in that room had this pen. While Ned might have left it somewhere accidentally, I saw him with it Thursday afternoon. So how did it get from him to here? There's a good chance the murderer is in there."

"There'll be so many prints on it, I don't see how it could be helpful."

"I know, but I'll still call Deputy Stanton."

Scott sighed. "You insist on being in the thick of things."

"Scott, you know Daniel was taken in for more questioning today."

We moved back to the edge of the light, now I had the pen put away.

"Yes, Michael told me. I helped arrange for the attorney to get to him."

"If you had seen his daughter crying, you'd know why I'm doing this. I promise I'm being careful, but I'll do everything I can to find Blaine's murderer."

"Okay, Kelly. What do you want to do now?"

"I want to go back in for a short while and be the happy guest. Then thank Roger and leave."

"All right. I doubt anyone is going to be alarmed about the pen missing. Since it was being passed around, whoever had it wasn't concerned about the pen. However, I want to escort you to your car and follow you back to the inn."

"Scott—"

"It's only a few minutes out of the way for me. I'll feel better watching you walk into the building and close the door behind you...and lock it."

I wanted to protest, but more than that, I wanted to get moving.

"I appreciate your concern."

We walked back in together and heard Roger hit his crystal gong a few times. The drawing was about to begin.

"Any more names for the basket?" Roger glanced around at the eager crowd.

People shook their heads and no one stepped forward.

"I've asked Phil, our wine sommelier, to give a brief description of the wines and to pick the names."

Phil held up a bottle with a gold label and proceeded to give a couple of sentences of wine talk. He ran his fingers around in the basket and pulled a name. "Elise Jenkins," he declared.

Elise gave a "Yippee!" of delight and claimed her prize.

Peter gave her a hug when she got back to him.

After another brief wine description, Phil chose the next name. "Kelly Jackson!"

Totally surprised, I walked forward.

Phil handed me the bottle. "Congratulations, Kelly."

He continued through the process until all the wine was claimed. Scott stayed with me as I touched base with some of the people I'd met earlier. I introduced Scott to the ones he didn't know. When I was ready to leave, I went to thank Roger and say good-bye.

"Kelly, thank you for your help with the drawing."

He was a difficult man to read. Was it a warm thank you or an inquisitive assessment in his eyes?

"It was a great success," I said.

"Seems like it."

"Thank you for the wonderful time. I'm going to excuse myself. I have a meeting in the morning and some preparation work I need to do."

Time to update the charts.

"Thank you for coming." He turned to Scott and shook his hand. "Good to see you again. I'll be hiring your people for more events in the future."

"I'm glad to hear it. I'll let them know."

I reclaimed my jacket and Scott stayed with me while the valets went to get our vehicles. He offered to hold my bottle of wine as I put on my parka and zipped it up to ward off the onset of the chilly night air.

The cars arrived one after the other.

"I'll be right behind you," Scott said.

"Okay."

He followed me home and walked me to the back door.

"I'll wait until I hear the click of the lock."

I laughed. "You *are* thorough."

"I don't want Murphy's Law to be in effect and find out later the lock decided not to work."

I nodded and smiled. "I understand."

He started to say something else, then one of the guests drove in.

We said good night. I went in, locked the door, and gave him a wave through the window. He smiled and trotted down the stairs. I did a routine check of the parlor. The fire was almost out.

I swung by the study and put the pen in the office safe.

I went to my rooms and pulled my phone out to call Stanton, then saw a text from Corrigan. He'd planned on coming next week but had rearranged his schedule and would be arriving tomorrow morning. He'd be by as soon as he could make it. I texted Daniel to let him know.

I called Stanton and told him I had what I believed to be Ned Blaine's pen and how it had come into my possession. He felt like Scott and I that, with so many people handling it, it was unlikely he'd get anything of value from it. He said he'd come by tomorrow and pick it up. I told him I'd put it behind the bottom step of the back porch.

"Elise and Joey made an appointment with me, and I talked with them this afternoon," Stanton said. "I know who bumped into you and put you in the water."

"Who?" I almost shouted.

"Joey."

It made no sense. Why push me in then pull me out?

Chapter 26

"Why did he do it?"

"Not a why, according to him. He said he stumbled and accidentally bumped into you. He was too embarrassed to tell you. Personally, I'm not buying it. I'd watch myself around him, if I were you. Since he also saved you and no one actually saw the incident, there's nothing I can charge him with."

The deputy said he'd talked to some of the guides and they told him Joey had been near the area where I went in, but no one had witnessed him pushing me. Stanton told Joey he planned to question the rest of the guides, and if someone saw him shove me, he'd take action. That was when Joey confessed to the accidental push into the river.

"It was a pretty clever move on his part to tell me he did it," Stanton said. "I doubt if anyone would've been close enough to be able to tell the difference between a bump and a push. He did a good job of covering himself."

He went on to tell me what else had transpired. Elise had kept her word and she and Joey had talked about the blackmailing by Ned Blaine.

"I'm telling you about Joey being blackmailed because Elise says she talked with you about it. I'm not at liberty to give you any other information I received about the blackmailing."

"I understand. She told me this afternoon."

I didn't mention she had contacted him at my insistence or that the conversation took place before he arrived.

We ended the call, and I turned in for the night, with many questions and few answers on my mind.

The next morning I retrieved Ned's pen and put it behind the back porch step for Deputy Stanton to pick up. Helen and I made quick work of cleaning up baskets and leftover breakfast food. I let her know Corrigan was coming and could show up at any time.

Helen put the last of the dishes in the washer. "Tommy, Allie, and I are going to the festival presentations in town. Priscilla's owner said she'd be there, and the kids want to see her again."

"I plan on being there as well."

I headed for the conference room, wanting to update the information before Corrigan arrived. I added finding the pen and Roger not being the note deliverer on the "other" chart. After "Joey" I wrote *accidental river pushing* with a question mark, *being blackmailed*, and *finding the body*. I wondered if the others would have anything to contribute. Helen brought in the usual refreshments and the room was ready for the meeting.

Andy and Phil texted as promised. Unfortunately, neither of them had heard or seen anything they thought would further our investigation.

The Silver Sentinels began to arrive and soon everyone was assembled.

Mary placed a box of doughnuts sprinkled with powdered sugar on the table. "It's been ages since I've made these. I found the process relaxing—something I needed. There's homemade raspberry jam in the middle."

The sweet smell of the treats filled the room.

Mary took Princess out of her carrier, along with a small pink blanket, put the dog on the floor, then made a bed for her in the corner.

The group helped themselves to treats and beverages. As soon as everyone was settled, Gertie started the meeting. I went over my additions and asked if they had discovered anything more. I didn't mention my agreement with Elise.

"I have something," the Professor said. "The Fungi Finders are taking turns staking out the area being illegally logged. They didn't like the idea of someone stealing the public's trees."

Gertie nodded. "Good. I hope they catch them."

The Professor added, "I have no idea if there's any connection with the logging and Ned Blaine's murder."

Rudy frowned. "I wonder if Ned Blaine was blackmailing the people taking the wood."

"That's a possibility," I said. "He was clearly into other people's business."

"I didn't get anywhere with Elise yesterday afternoon," Mary said. "The woman was in no mood to talk."

And I know why.

Rudy, Ivan, and Gertie had nothing to add.

I filled them in on Daniel's questioning, the arrival of the attorney, and Allie's distress.

Mary put down the knitting she'd started. "Poor girl. I wish we could solve this and have it over with."

The Professor nodded. "I couldn't agree more. However, we must remember the murder happened three nights ago, and we've only had two full days to work on it. We've already gathered quite a bit of information."

They nodded and agreed to carry on with the plans they'd generated yesterday, slim though they were.

"Michael Corrigan is arriving this morning. He planned to visit next week, but he moved his trip up," I said.

"Such a nice man," Mary said. "He'll be getting an earful of thank-yous for the community center."

"I thought I'd go over to see the contest awards this morning," I said. "Both to be supportive and because maybe I'll hear or see something useful."

"Excellent idea, my dear," the Professor said. "I think we should all go."

There was a perceptual brightening in the group at the thought of a new action plan.

"I'd like to meet at noon to see if we've found out anything," I said.

Mary nodded. "Even if it's only a speck here and there, something might connect the dots and move us forward."

The others agreed.

My phone pinged, and I saw a message from Michael saying he'd arrived at the inn. I let him know we were in the conference room.

A few minutes later, my boss entered. My first thought at seeing him was always lumberjack, never billionaire. He had the build of someone with a physically demanding job. The red plaid flannel shirt and blue jeans spoke country, not big city. I'd seen him in custom-tailored Italian suits when the situation called for it, but his preference was casual.

Before the Sentinels could gather round him, Princess raced out of her corner, ran under the table, and charged out barking.

Michael laughed and bent down on one knee. The tan Chihuahua slid to a stop and put both her front paws on Michael's leg.

He gently petted her, his hand larger than the little dog's head. "Who is this cutie?"

"Princess," Mary promptly replied. "She's my sister's retired hearing assistance dog. We both raised her. When my sister moved and got another dog, she stayed with me."

He scratched Princess behind her right ear. "The name fits with all the rhinestones in her collar and on her sweater. Clothing befitting royalty."

He got to his feet and the Sentinels proceeded with their warm welcome. He responded in kind.

"Michael," the Professor said, "we all want you to know how honored we are to have this room named after us."

"You're welcome, and thank you for all the lovely notes of appreciation. It was a small thing for me to do, considering how much you've done for the community, as well as for my staff and me personally."

"We're putting the laptops you gave us to good use," Gertie said. "They helped a lot on our last case."

"Glad to hear it."

He turned to me. "I texted Daniel so he and I could get together and talk after the meeting. I told him where we were." Then he began to look at our charts. "I see you've been busy like usual."

He scanned the information and asked questions. It took him only a short while to get up to speed.

He walked over to one chart and pointed to a couple of spots. "Kelly, what's this about you being pushed into a river and receiving a threatening note?"

I explained, downplaying it as much as I could.

"I see you have the name of the person who put you in the river. Why is there a question mark after the word *accidental*?"

"Deputy Stanton said he didn't buy Joey's explanation."

"As I've said in the past, he has a good handle on people, so I'd believe him."

"I agree."

Michael shook his head. "I'm sure glad I hired you to manage an inn in the quiet, safe town of Redwood Cove. Are you sure you don't want to go back to your troubleshooting position? You never dealt with this much when you were intentionally looking into problems."

"I'm sure. This is my home now. I love the area and have wonderful new friends."

The Silver Sentinels beamed.

Before I could add more, Daniel appeared in the doorway.

"Come on in," Michael said.

He entered, followed by Allie. "Michael, this is my daughter, Allie."

"Hello, Allie." Michael held out his hand.

She took it with her small, slender one. "Mr. Corrigan, I want to thank you for helping my dad."

I could see tears in the corners of her eyes.

Corrigan patted the top of her hand. "People who work for me are part of my family. I want them to be there for each other. I'll always do whatever I can to help."

A tear trickled down her cheek. She wiped it away with her palm.

"I made this for you." She handed him a card made from blue construction paper and adorned with small gold stars.

He read it aloud. "'Thank you for helping my dad. I love him very much. You're a wonderful person.'" Michael smiled at Allie. "That's very touching."

He held it up, and we could see the message as well as a photo of a bald eagle she had glued to the left side. The bird stood on a branch facing us, tall and proud. Its light yellow eyes seemed to stare directly at us down its orange hooked beak—fierce and challenging. There was a good reason the bald eagle had been chosen as a symbol for our country.

"I pasted a picture of a bald eagle on the card because I've read they're very powerful spiritual guides and they symbolize freedom and victory," Allie explained. "You kept my dad free."

Daniel put his hand on his daughter's shoulder. "Allie and I did a ceremony this morning and prayed for the police to have victory in finding Ned Blaine's killer."

"I have a gift for you," Allie said to Michael and held up a feather. "I found this eagle feather on a hike with my dad. I want you to have it." She handed it to Corrigan.

"I'm honored, Allie." Michael examined the feather. "It's beautiful, but what's more important than its appearance is its meaning. I'll mount it on a wall in my den to always be a reminder of you and your father."

She smiled at him and took her father's hand.

Michael held up the feather. "To freedom and victory."

We all cheered.

I looked at the clock and realized we needed to get going if we were going to make it to the town center for the contest awards. I shared with Michael and Daniel what we were planning.

"I might join you later," Michael said. "Right now I want to talk with Daniel."

Allie said good-bye to her dad and went to join Helen and Tommy. Rudy and Ivan chose to walk to town, while the Professor planned to chauffer Gertie and Mary.

I drove the inn's truck and parked near the judging area. As I walked to where the presentation was going to be, I saw Elise, Peter, and Joey, with plates full of pancakes, settle themselves at a wooden table.

Two rows of colorful woven mushroom-collecting baskets rested on the platform. Roger was at the lectern with a handful of stapled papers. He waved me over.

"Kelly, I have a big favor to ask. I just realized I forgot the carved mushroom prizes I showed you. Probably lack of sleep catching up with me. There's no one I can call at the house to bring them because I gave all of my staff the day off. They've been working long days because of the two parties I put on. I have a speech to give. Would you be willing to go get them?"

"Sure. Are the awards where I saw them when I visited?"

He took a ring of keys out of his pocket and handed them to me. "Yes. I haven't moved them." He pulled out his wallet, extracted a card, and gave it to me. "That's the code for the gate."

I bet one of the keys opens the workshop. Maybe I can see what is in there. "I'll be back as fast as I can."

"Thanks. I really appreciate it." Roger walked over to where the mayor was standing.

I walked quickly to the truck. Three of the four suspects were just starting to eat breakfast and the fourth was going to be in front of a crowd giving a speech.

I'd be safe.

Chapter 27

I drove to Roger's house, opened the gate, and went up the now familiar driveway. Parking in front of the gallery, I took the keys he'd given me out of my pocket and unlocked the door. I could see the awards where he'd left them, but my focus was on the work area.

There were five keys on the ring. The third one did the trick. I opened the door and shoved the keys in my pocket. Dank, musty air assaulted my senses. I flipped on the lights, and there it was. The huge log had to be the one from the river. It rested on several thick blocks of wood. Heavy-duty chains were wrapped around it in several places.

I walked up to it and placed my hand on the cold, damp surface. Old-growth redwood. It could be over two thousand years old.

"Roger must have wanted you pretty badly," I said softly.

"Yes, I did," a voice said behind me.

Fear shot through me. I stiffened and slowly turned. Roger stood in the doorway.

"It doesn't look like much now, but someday it will produce many one-of-a-kind objects."

"What happened with your speech?"

My voice shook.

"Actually, the mayor was giving the speech, not me." He inclined his head toward the gallery display area. "Come here. I want to show you something."

I knew there was only one way to get in the work area...that meant there was only one way out. Maybe I could escape out the front somehow. I gulped and walked with robot-stiff steps toward him. He turned and entered the front room. I kept a good distance between us and stopped just inside the studio.

Roger picked up a remote control. "Do you want to see what you look like on television?"

What on earth was he talking about?

He pointed his remote to a television mounted to the ceiling in the corner of the room. Roger clicked a button, and it sprang to life, showing the front of the gallery at night. I recognized the inn's truck. . . and then I got to see myself searching for lights and cameras…and then going around the side of the building. There I was with my flashlight trying to see inside. He had multiple hidden cameras.

I swallowed hard. "Why the concealed cameras?" It was more of a squeak than a question.

"I don't want to scare people away with motion lights or obvious surveillance equipment. I like to know who's sneaking around my property… so I can take care of them."

I was sure he didn't mean taking care of them in a nice way.

I backed up a step.

His eyes were cold. "I get rid of the problems in my life."

And I was a problem.

I took another step back.

Roger put the remote down, reached in a drawer, took out a gun, and pointed it at me.

I had difficulty breathing. "You'd…you'd kill me for a log?" I managed to stammer.

"No, there are a couple of reasons. There's a chance I'd be arrested, although I was careful. Peter hired the additional men and equipment. I gave him cash for the transactions."

I felt queasy. "Joey said it's usually just a fine and they take the log."

"This is different. It's on a much larger scale and on federal property. We couldn't help but damage the area. I'd probably get off with just a fine, but I don't deal in probablys."

I was trembling uncontrollably. "Are you going to kill Joey and Peter too because they know about the theft?"

"No. I'm not worried about them. They did the actual stealing and would be in more trouble than me. Also, that log will need a lot of work, and they'll be the ones to do it. I'm their meal ticket for a long time to come."

Buy time. Buy time. "You said a couple of reasons."

"If the Feds find out I have it, they'll confiscate it. It's the only one like it that exists. Believe me, I've looked."

I believed him.

"It's priceless. Money can't buy anything like it. Peter's puny little logs, and he only had a few of those, made me want it even more."

Time. I need more time. "Did you kill Ned Blaine?"

"No reason not to tell you. You won't be here much longer. Yes, I did. I met with Joey that night to finalize his part in the plan for taking the log. Blaine had followed Joey. Joey left before me because I didn't want us seen together, and he never saw the reporter."

I willed myself to stop shaking. "But why kill him?"

"He wanted money to keep quiet. Kept waving a stupid pen in my face. I grabbed it and shoved it in my pocket." His lips smiled, but his eyes didn't. "I saw you take it, by the way—at the party. There's no proof of who had it, and there'll be way too many prints for it to be useful."

More answers, not that they helped me any.

"I probably could've handled it another way, found a way to blackmail him back for his silence. But men and equipment were lined up and he'd been making life miserable for a lot of people. So I shot him. End of problem."

Roger tightened his grip on the gun. "I'm sorry I have to do this. I liked you, except for your snooping around. With all the questions you've been asking, it was clear you didn't plan to stop."

Fear paralyzed me.

My knees began to buckle.

I had to do something.

I rammed into the display table next to me, knocking several sculptures to the ground, dashing them to pieces.

Roger cried out as he looked at his shattered artwork, distracted for an instant.

I twirled around, ran through the work area door, and locked it behind me. I looked around, searching for a way out I hadn't seen previously, a place to hide, or something I could use as a weapon. Bullets began hitting the door and the lock. Splinters flew in every direction. A few hit my face, causing a stinging pain.

I frantically searched for something to jam the door closed. In a corner I saw the forklift I'd seen on my earlier visit. I'd driven similar equipment on the ranch.

I ran toward it, searching the key ring with trembling fingers. I found one that looked right. Crawling into the driver's seat, I inserted it, turned the key, and said a silent thank-you as the engine came to life. I shoved it into gear and drove it to the door, ramming the prongs against it.

The door handle turned, but the door didn't open.

Roger's voice came over the sound of the engine. "Whatever you've done, it won't keep me from getting you. You have nowhere to go, and there's no one here to help you. I don't get unexpected visitors…and cell phones don't work here."

The door began shaking as he threw his weight against it.

He was right. I knew a padlock secured the barn doors, and he had the key. The windows were barred. His property was isolated, and, with no people on-site, there was no one to hear me scream. All he had to do was figure a way to block the door on his side and then come in the back way. He had all the time in the world to figure out how to do that. I was a sitting duck.

I needed to get to him first. Catch him off guard. Blood pounded in my ears.

I threw the forklift into reverse and backed up. Roger hit the door again and it sprang open. He fell through the doorway from the lack of resistance, firing at me as he went down.

I ducked, put the forklift in gear, and hit the accelerator, aiming for Roger. I would run him down if I had to. Roger had gotten to his feet and jumped back, but not before a prong sliced the side of his left leg.

Roger screamed and twirled around. Blood gushed from the wound. I turned the forklift toward him. He dodged the metal blades, but one of the large tires caught him on the shoulder. Roger flew backward, arms flung out, his head hitting a worktable. The gun flew out of his hand as he dropped to the floor, motionless.

I jumped out of the cab and grabbed the gun. I knew how to use a gun and wouldn't hesitate if Roger tried anything. Backing into the studio, I spotted a phone on the wall next to the door. With my gaze never leaving Roger and the gun aimed at him, I took the receiver off the wall with my left hand and punched in 911.

The police were on their way.

It wasn't long before I heard a siren getting louder as it neared. Roger never moved.

The shrill wail went silent and an officer came in, gun drawn. I lowered Roger's gun then knelt and put it on the floor.

"I'm Deputy Sheriff Clark." He went to Roger and checked his pulse. "Are you okay?"

I nodded. "Shaken, but other than a few splinters, I'm fine."

"All members of the department are up-to-date on what's been happening. I know the background of Ned Blaine's murder case."

I explained what had happened. Roger remained motionless. Other officers arrived and an ambulance was summoned.

Deputy Clark closed his notebook. "There'll be some details to work out, but basically it's case closed. Nice to have it over with."

Case closed. I liked the sound of that.

"I couldn't agree more," I said with relish.

"You're free to go. We'll be in touch if we need anything."

"Thanks."

I walked to my vehicle. At least the case of who killed Ned Blaine was solved. But there were still questions to be answered. Had Roger been the one to poison Clarence? I wondered if they'd ever find out. And who put the threatening note on my car?

I got in my truck, pulled the keys out of my pocket, and started it. It took some maneuvering to get through all the police cars. I heard the sound of an approaching siren and saw the ambulance headed up the driveway. I drove over to the side of the road to give them room to get by.

I looked at myself in the rearview mirror. The splinters had left a few spots of blood on my face but hadn't embedded themselves. I took a clean tissue out of the box I kept in the glove compartment and poured a little water on it from my water bottle. A few swipes and people wouldn't know there were some pinpoint cuts.

As soon as the ambulance was past me, I took off. I was anxious to tell Daniel and the others the murderer had been caught. I knew where my cell phone would begin working and parked on the shoulder of the road and called Daniel. I wanted to tell him personally. No answer. I texted him a brief message, saying the killer had been caught.

I pulled back onto the road and drove to town, where the Mushroom Festival activities were taking place. As I parked, I saw Deputy Sheriff Stanton walking across the town center, along with two other officers. He must already know, but I wanted to be sure. It was cause for celebration.

The policemen walked to where Elise, Peter, and Joey sat. I got there just as they arrived at the table. Anxious looks passed between the three seated there.

"Peter Smith and Joey Jenkins, I'm placing you under arrest for illegal logging."

"What are you taking about?" Peter spat out.

"A local mushroom club decided to stake out the area where redwoods have been cut down. They marked some trees so they could be identified. They called and told us they'd seen you two at work. We obtained a search warrant and found the wood in your barn."

Peter seemed to shrink as the bluster and bravado left him.

"And you, Elise Jenkins, are under arrest for the attempted murder of Clarence Norton."

Chapter 28

Elise paled. "No…wait…"

Peter jumped up. "You have it all wrong, Deputy Stanton. I was the one who put the mushrooms in the salad. I wanted to make him sick so he and his stupid dog would quit the contest. I never meant to kill him."

Elise looked stunned. "What? You put those mushrooms there?"

"Yeah. I didn't mean to cause you any grief, Elise." Peter put his hand on hers. "I'm sorry. I thought people would figure the guy ate some of his own mushrooms that were poisonous."

Stanton cleared his throat. "Elise, all the people at the dinner said you were the only one they saw near the entrée. We found poisonous mushrooms in what was left of Clarence's dinner."

"What?" Peter exclaimed, staring at her. "You poisoned him, too?"

Elise nodded. "Joey saw Clarence Thursday night when Joey was meeting with the person who pays him to retrieve sinker logs. He didn't know if Clarence saw him or not, and I wanted to make him sick so he'd leave."

"Okay," Deputy Stanton said. "Let's see if I've got this straight. You both poisoned him but neither of you meant to kill him. Because there were two portions of poisonous mushrooms, it became life threatening. Neither of you knew what the other one was up to."

They nodded in unison.

Stanton shoved his hat back on his head. "A fine pair you are." He pulled out handcuffs. "It's still a criminal offense to intentionally poison someone."

Peter and Elise shared frightened looks.

"Elise, we also got a search warrant for your place, since you were a murder suspect. We found the remnants of the pages you used to create the warning note to Kelly Jackson. They were a perfect match."

Elise's shoulders sagged. "I wanted her to quit asking so many questions. I thought it might make the others in her group stop as well. I knew about the illegal logging and the sinker logs. I figured it was only a matter of time before she or the others found out something that would harm Peter or Joey."

I stepped forward. "Excuse me, Deputy Sheriff Stanton. Is it okay for me to ask a question? There's one incident left to clear up."

"Yes, Ms. Jackson. If something else can be solved, that's a good thing."

I looked at Elise. "Why did Joey push me in the water and then save me? I know he said it was an accident, but I don't believe that. I won't press charges against you for the note or Joey if he shoved me in the river. I just want the truth."

"Can she do that, Deputy Stanton?" Elise asked.

"It's her choice," he replied.

It was a small trade to make to get all the answers. She'd still face charges regarding Clarence and, besides the logging, I knew Joey and Peter would have the stolen sinker log to deal with.

Joey shot his mother a look.

Elise turned back to me. "You promise you won't press charges?"

"You know I keep my word, Elise."

She blushed a bit. "We wanted to scare you, not kill you. He stuck around in case you couldn't swim and he'd have to go in and save you."

There it was. The last answer to all of our questions.

"Thank you, Deputy Stanton."

He nodded and opened the handcuffs.

I walked away. Now wasn't the time to talk to him. I saw Priscilla and Ted surrounded by a group that included the Silver Sentinels, Helen, Daniel, and the kids, as well as Fred on a leash. The pig pawed twice with her front right hoof, then twice with her left—a tap dance on the concrete sidewalk. I felt like dancing along with her.

I merged with the group and stood next to Daniel. He had his arm around Allie's shoulders.

He smiled at me. "Hi, Kelly."

"Hi, back. Have you checked your phone recently?"

He looked at me quizzically, reached in his pocket, and took out his cell phone. The shine of his smile after reading the text put the finishing touch on the day. I asked if he could meet at the inn in an hour, and I'd tell him what had happened. He said yes. I did the same with the Sentinels, and they said they would be there, after happy exclamations when they heard the murderer was caught.

I saw Stanton and the other officers, with their three arrestees, headed for patrol cars. I texted Michael the news and said we'd be meeting in an hour at the inn if he wanted to join us. He replied immediately he'd be there.

Clapping drew my attention to the stage. A young woman held a blue ribbon, along with her colorful mushroom basket.

A chubby man in a plaid judge's vest said, "Again, congratulations on the most artistic basket. Now, we want to award the Judge's Choice. This can be for anything the judges deem noteworthy. This year we're awarding it for most entertaining contestant. The winner is…Priscilla the pig!"

People applauded and whistled. The black-and-white pig trotted onto the stage, Ted in tow, tail wiggling, her movements punctuated with grunts and squeals. I saw the announcer place a bundle of corn ears tied with a ribbon on the table next to the podium.

I wondered what they'd say when it came time to award the mushroom winners and there were no prizes. I wasn't interested enough to wait around and find out. I said good-bye to the group.

I took my time driving back to the inn, pulling over at one point to gaze at the deep blue ocean. It was calm today. There were always waves, but today they were gentle. The turbulence of the last few days began to slip away as I watched their rhythmic movement. I took in a deep breath of fresh coastal air and realized I hadn't been aware of it the last couple of days.

I drove to the inn and parked. I entered the now quiet kitchen, glad for some silent time and a chance to process what happened today. I'd not go into great detail about my fight with Roger when I talked with everyone. I'd had a close call. I went to my room, washed up, and checked my face in the mirror. The splinter specks hadn't bled anymore.

I saw a few slivers attached to my jeans and changed. I brushed my hair and put some lotion on my hands. I was moving at a languid pace, as if my body wanted to balance the adrenaline rush of the morning. A sense of moving in slow motion replaced the rapid-fire action I'd experienced.

I put together a tray of beverages and took it to the Silver Sentinels' Conference Room. Being able to do mundane tasks was a pleasure. I'd come close to not being able to do them again. I scanned the charts. All the answers. Finally.

The Silver Sentinels began to arrive. They were early, probably wanting to hear the details as soon as possible. Ivan punched Rudy lightly on the shoulder. He was in a playful mood.

Mary put the Princess purse on a chair and lifted out her pride and joy. No sweet treats for the group, probably forgotten in her rush to hear the conclusion to our efforts. Today's news was sweet enough.

The Professor came in, keeping pace with Gertie and her cane. Using it never seemed to slow her down. Daniel was right behind them.

Corrigan came in...followed by Scott. There definitely wouldn't be a lot of detail in my report, considering his level of concern. People settled with their drinks, and I began to tell the story.

Ivan got up and grabbed a thick, black marking pen and went to the charts. "I check off."

With each issue I addressed, he checked it off with a flourish. When I was done, everything had been covered.

Job done.

No one had said anything when I told what had happened with Roger. However, the somber faces and serious glances at each other spoke volumes.

I could see Corrigan reading the charts.

"All of you accomplished a lot," he said. "Once again, a boon to this community."

"We feel it's important to help in any way we can," the Professor said.

Michael surveyed the group. "Kelly had a close call." He looked at me. "I suppose asking you and the others not to do anything like this again would be a waste of my breath."

We all nodded.

"Daniel was in danger," I said. "I don't regret what I did for an instant. I'd do it for anyone in this room."

The Silver Sentinels agreed with me.

"I didn't know what I was getting into when I hired a Wyoming cowgirl," Michael remarked.

The shared laughter eased the tension that had built in the room when I told them what had happened at Roger's place.

Daniel sat back. "I know I, for one, feel like a celebration is in order. It's time for triple hot chocolate for the kids and an extra big pizza party tonight. This is our Sunday family night at Redwood Cove Bed-and-Breakfast, and you're all invited to join us."

I chimed in. "And I have a fine bottle of merlot, thanks to Roger Simmons. There's enough for each of us to make a toast."

The Sentinels weren't ones to be left out. Gertie offered a salad, and Mary said she'd bring dessert. Rudy, Ivan, and the Professor said they'd bring drinks. When Michael and Scott offered to bring something, the others vetoed them and said there'd be plenty.

I texted Stanton and invited him. I wondered if I'd ever get used to thinking of him as Bill. Maybe when we weren't involved in police business. He said he'd be there.

We agreed to meet at five. The Professor shared the news that Clarence had been released from the hospital. I encouraged him to ask Clarence and Timothy to join us. He said he would.

Scott lingered behind after the others left. "Kelly, I know you're not going to change. I won't try to discourage you. I'm glad you weren't hurt."

I began to take the charts down. "Thanks, Scott."

"Please remember to let me help in any way if there's another investigation you get involved in...though I'd like to think Redwood Cove is done with crime."

"Me, too. And yes, I'll remember your offer *if* I ever need it."

The rest of the afternoon passed quickly, and soon people began to arrive, including Timothy and Clarence. Mary put the Princess blanket next to Fred's bed between the two beanbag chairs in the living area. After a few doggie hellos to people, Princess curled up and closed her eyes.

Clarence came into the kitchen, where I was talking with Daniel. "I'm...I'm so sorry for following you two."

I didn't think anyone could blush as red as I usually did, but Clarence proved me wrong.

"At the time, I had mushrooms on my mind and didn't think of it as spying." He got even redder.

It was interesting to watch the crimson tide instead of being the one to provide the show.

"Please forgive me," Clarence said.

I patted him on the shoulder. "Of course. I'm guessing we've all had times when we've regretted our actions. Glad you could join us tonight."

Daniel nodded. "I'm with Kelly. You learned from it and now it's time to move on and let it go."

"Thank you both so much. Never again, for sure." He held up an empty plastic bottle. "I'd like to get some water for Max."

"Go ahead," I said. "I'd like to see him again."

Clarence filled the bottle, and I followed him out. He opened the back of his pickup and there was the golden-curled Max...wearing his service vest. It seemed Clarence had decided to take a new direction in dealing with his disease.

I petted the regal dog while Clarence filled his water bowl. "Do you want to bring him in?"

"No. He's tuckered out from all the excitement of the last couple days. A long nap will be good for him."

Deputy Stanton's patrol car pulled in and parked next to Clarence's vehicle.

"Can't stay long," he said. "But I do need to take a dinner break."

We went in and joined the others. Everyone was there. Happy conversation filled the air.

Tommy raced into the room, with Fred close on his heels. "Everyone, look."

We all stopped talking and gave Tommy and Fred center stage.

Tommy stood up tall. "Fred, roll over." He made a motion with his hand.

Fred blinked a couple of times, crouched down in slow motion, and rolled his tub of a body over. No easy feat. Everyone clapped. Fred jumped up much faster than he went down, his tail wagging furiously. He went to his bed, climbed in, and settled next to Princess.

The delivery of five extra-large pizzas signaled party time. There'd be leftovers for sure. We did our toast and said good-bye and good riddance to Roger, then filled our plates with pizza and salad. People chose their seats at the table or the counter divider.

Michael pulled a slice dripping with cheese from the pizza box. "The attorney is headed home as he is no longer needed to help Daniel."

What wonderful words those were to hear.

"However, he's working for me on another project." Michael looked over at Daniel. "I'm going to fund the repair of the sacred land that was destroyed during the removal of the log."

"Michael, thank you—"

Corrigan held up his hand. "I want your tribe to plan and participate in the work. There will be hoops to jump through, but I think I can swing it."

"The area means a lot to us. People will be proud to help reclaim it."

I helped myself to a slice with chicken and herbs on top. The day just kept getting better and better.

Stanton—that is, Bill—sat between Helen and Tommy, chewing a piece of pepperoni pizza. Maybe there was a new beginning waiting for Helen.

The words *bocce ball* and *fly fishing* drifted over from where Clarence and Timothy conversed. Sounded like plans for their next competition were under way.

Scott sat next to me. "Are you still up for cooking lessons?"

"I am indeed."

He arched an eyebrow and tilted his head. "Would Tuesday afternoon work?"

"Yes," I replied.

"We'll start with mac and cheese, but not just any old mac and cheese. I'll give you a hint—I got the cheese from Andy."

I knew that meant gourmet.

Maybe there was something new for me on the horizon as well.

We all ate contentedly and chatted. The conversations held no talk of murder.

Tommy stood and put his plate in the sink, then went to the inn's computer. A couple of minutes later, he shouted, "Mom! Mom!"

Helen laughed. "I'm right here, honey. You don't have to be so loud."

He pushed some buttons on the computer and a sheet of paper came out of the printer. Tommy raced to his mother with it.

"It's my first cookie order. It's for a dozen bulldog cookies. The dog's name is Maude."

He held her picture up for everyone to see. "It's going to be fun making all the wrinkles on her face."

His first custom cookie order...and Daniel would be there to make the mold. I loved my new family and Redwood Cove. Now things could return to normal—though I was beginning to wonder what normal was for this seaside village.

About the Author

Janet Finsilver and her husband live in the San Francisco Bay Area. She loves animals and has two dogs—Kylie, a Rhodesian ridgeback, and Ellie, a boxer/coonhound mix. Janet enjoys horseback riding, snow skiing, and cooking. She is currently working on her next Redwood Cove mystery. Readers can visit her website at www.JanetFinsilver.com.

Printed in the United States
by Baker & Taylor Publisher Services